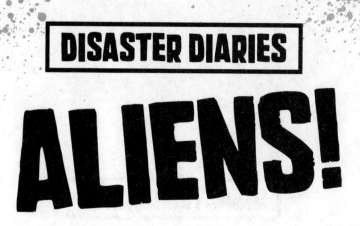

DISASTER DIARIES

ALIENS!

DISASTER DIARIES

Zombies!

Aliens!

Brainwashed!

DISASTER DIARIES

ALIENS!

R. McGEDDON

ILLUSTRATED BY JAMIE LITTLER

【Imprint】

MAKE YOUR MARK

NEW YORK

Special thanks to Barry Hutchison

[Imprint]
MAKE YOUR MARK

A part of Macmillan Children's Publishing Group

DISASTER DIARIES: ALIENS! Text copyright © 2014 by Hothouse Fiction Ltd. Illustrations copyright © 2014 by Jamie Littler. All rights reserved. Printed in the United States of America by R. R. Donnelley & Sons Company, Harrisonburg, Virginia. For information, address Imprint, 175 Fifth Avenue, New York, N.Y. 10010.

Sizzling in the fiery stars
Or lengthy banishment on Mars
Awaits the borrower of these pages
Who doesn't give it back for ages!

Library of Congress Cataloging-in-Publication Data is available.
ISBN 978-1-250-09088-1 (hardcover) / ISBN 978-1-250-09089-8 (ebook)

Our books may be purchased in bulk for promotional, educational, or business use. Please contact your local bookseller or the Macmillan Corporate and Premium Sales Department at (800) 221-7945 ext. 5442 or by e-mail at MacmillanSpecialMarkets@macmillan.com.

Imprint logo designed by Amanda Spielman

First published in Great Britain in 2014 by Little, Brown Books for Young Readers

First U.S. Edition—2016

10 9 8 7 6 5 4 3 2 1

mackids.com

FOR MR. T

CHAPTER ONE

Somewhere near the center of the town of Sitting Duck lies Hetchley's Park. It's quite nice. I mean, it's not brilliant, but, you know, it's all right. It's got a lake, which is pretty cool.

Okay, it's not actually a lake as such—it's a duck pond. But still, that's not bad, is it?

Right, fine, it doesn't have a duck pond, either. It has a bench. But it's a nice bench, and that's what counts. Geez, stop picking on Hetchley's Park. What's wrong with you?

Anyway, Hetchley's Park is near the middle of Sitting Duck, and near the middle of Hetchley's Park (just by the bench, which is actually in a bit of a state now that I look at it properly), best friends Sam, Arty, and Emmie were hanging out and having a laugh.

Or rather, Arty was having a laugh. The other two . . . not so much.

We'll come to that in a minute, though. First, let's take a closer look at the three friends. In alphabetical order, because everyone likes the alphabet, don't they?

Arty. He's a lovely lad, that Arty, if a bit too clever for his own good sometimes. People say that Arty's brain is as big as his belly, but that's clearly not true, because his head would have to be absolutely massive to hold a brain that size.

Emmie. *Pink*, *girly*, and *flowery*—three words that have never been used to describe Emmie. Of the three friends, Emmie is probably the toughest. She's an all-action girl who is rumored to have once punched a tiger in the face. Of course, the rumor is utter nonsense. She actually punched it in the ribs.

And finally we come to Sam. Everyone loves Sam. He's witty, charming, brave, and clever. Not *Arty* clever—no one's *Arty* clever

except Arty himself—but smart enough when he needs to be. He's just great all around, really. I mean, you should have seen how he handled the zombies in the last book. Wow. That's all I'm saying. Wow!

"Come on," giggled Arty, who was eager to get on with the story. "It's easy!"

Sam sighed. Emmie scowled. This treasure hunt Arty had set up had stopped being fun roughly four seconds after it had started. It was now entering its fifth hour. It was the code-breaking kit that was the problem. Arty had been given it for his birthday and thought it would be fun to leave cryptic clues for his friends to follow. Not for the first time that day, Sam wished Arty had just been given a football or something instead.

"Right, read the clue again," Sam said.

Emmie squinted at the rectangle of paper and read aloud:

RFC MJB MYI RPCC → 2

Sam nodded. "Right. So what does it mean?"

"How am I supposed to know?"

Arty snorted a laugh. "I can't believe you haven't figured it out. It's so easy!"

"I swear," growled Emmie, "say that one more time and you won't leave this park alive."

It was autumn, but the breeze that drifted around the park was warm. As it swept over Emmie, though, she gave a shiver. Her eyes darted across the grass, past the bench, and over to a clump of trees near the gate. This did not go unnoticed by Sam, because he's also quite sensitive, as well as all that other stuff I said about him earlier.

"You okay?" he asked.

"Of course I'm okay," Emmie snapped. She took a deep breath and her voice softened a little. "It's just . . . it's hard to believe it's been three months since . . ."

"The zombies," said Sam.

Emmie nodded.

"Poor Professor Pamplemousse," said Arty. "Apparently they found one of his arms wedged under the merry-go-round last month. It had been there the whole time."

"Nasty," said Sam. "I suppose he sort of brought it on himself, though. He did invent the zombie virus, after all."

"Not on purpose," said Arty.

Sam shrugged. "I suppose."

They stood in silence, each of them

remembering some of the horrors they'd seen over the summer. At least, Sam and Emmie were doing that. Arty had realized he had accidentally stepped on a massive dog poop and was trying to wipe it off on the grass without anyone noticing.

"Still, it's over now," said Sam.

"Is it?" asked Emmie. "Half the town still seems pretty brain-dead to me."

"They were always a bit like that," Sam reminded her. "Anyway, it's done with. Let's not talk about it anymore."

"Exactly!" cried Arty. "Not when we've got something much more fun to do instead!"

"Do we?" asked Emmie, hopefully. "Does that mean we can stop this stupid treasure hunt, then?"

Arty's face fell. "I was talking about the treasure hunt."

"You have a very strange concept of fun, my friend," said Emmie as she looked at the clue for about the fiftieth time since they'd arrived at the park. "Right, let's get this over with. It's a code, right? The groups of letters are words, so there are four words in the answer. Three with three letters, the last one with four."

"Correct!"

"What does the arrow mean?" asked Sam.

"Aha, if I told you that, you'd know the answer," Arty gloated. "You have to figure it out."

"Wait a minute," said Emmie. She turned to Sam. "The third clue. How did we figure that one out again?"

"No idea," admitted Sam. "I'd lost the will to live by then."

"Was that the one where the letters had been swapped with numbers?"

Arty giggled. "Might have been."

"Arty!" Emmie barked, so sharply she made both boys jump in fright.

"Okay, yes. That's right," Arty said quickly.

Sam peered at the clue. "But this one doesn't have numbers."

"No, but what if the letters have been swapped with other letters, and the arrow means move along?" Emmie suggested. So *A* would become *B*, *B* would become *C*. Like that."

"Only there's a number two, so—"

"You move two places instead!" Emmie realized. "Pass me a pencil, quick."

Sam fished in his pocket until he found the pencil Arty had given them at the start of the treasure hunt. It had been brand-new when Arty had handed it over, but now it was chewed all the way around, and Emmie had snapped it in half in a fit of rage twenty minutes into clue number one.

Silently, she scribbled on the paper right beneath Arty's studiously neat writing. As she wrote, a smile of relief spread across her face.

"'The Old Oak Tree,'" she read. "That's the final clue. The Old Oak Tree."

She grabbed Sam by the shoulders and squeezed. "We're almost there," she said, her voice a hysterical whisper. "We've almost done it. We're almost free. Quickly—to the Old Oak Tree!"

With a whoop of triumph, she raced off. A moment later, she raced back. "Where's the Old Oak Tree?" she asked.

Sam shrugged. "No idea."

"So it seems your search isn't over quite yet!" Arty laughed. He stopped abruptly when Emmie grabbed him by the front of his T-shirt and snarled right up in his face. "It's in my garden," he blurted.

Emmie's face darkened. "But that's back where we started."

"I know," Arty squeaked. "Funny, eh?"

"Right, that's it," Emmie replied. "I'm going to kill him."

Sam stepped between them. "Come on, Emmie, you can't kill him. It's his birthday."

"Thanks, Sam," wheezed Arty.

"Kill him tomorrow instead."

"Good idea," said Emmie. "Now, let's get to that oak tree and get this whole horrible ordeal over and done with."

☆ ☆ ☆

Arty's Treasure
Hunt Clues

These are just some of the more infuriating clues Arty set out for Sam and Emmie to solve. Each and every one of the below caused Emmie to inflict actual physical harm upon Arty's person.

Warning: Any attempt to solve them yourself may cause your head to implode, so best not to bother.

1. 20-8-5 3-12-21-5 9-19 9-14 19-1-13 19
   12-5-6-20 19-8-15-5

(Use numbers instead of letters.)

2. --- -. / .- / -.. --- --. .-.-.- / .- -. -.-- / -.. --- --. .-.-.-

(Nothing beats Morse code.)

3. Apple, cherry, and rhubarb are some examples. Get past the point and take the fourth numeral to the place of nightmares.

(The more surreal the better.)

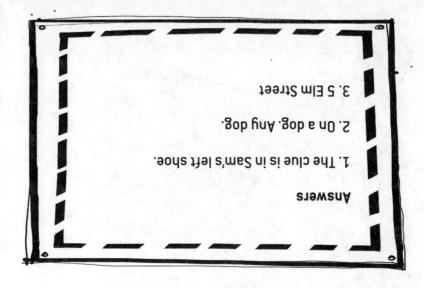

Sam had climbed the big tree in Arty's garden hundreds of times in the past but had never known it was an oak. Come on, give the guy a break. I said he was great; I never said he was perfect.

He and Emmie squeezed through the narrow gap in Arty's back fence, then spent a good fifteen minutes trying to pull Arty behind them. For a horrible moment halfway through, it looked like Arty was going to be stuck there, wedged in the gap forever, until Emmie climbed back over

the fence
and shoulder-
barged him through
from behind.

The towering oak tree loomed
above; up there was the tree house Arty
had built himself to hide from his big brother,
Jesse. The three friends climbed quickly up the

thick trunk. The end of the treasure hunt was in sight, and Sam and Emmie had never been so happy in their entire lives.

"It's a shame it's over," puffed Arty as he heaved himself up onto a higher branch.

"No, it isn't," said Emmie.

"She's right," agreed Sam. "No offense, but I'd rather face the zombies again than another one of those clues."

"This treasure had better be worth it—that's all I'm saying," Emmie said as she heaved herself in through the tree house window. Sam slid in behind her. A moment later, Arty came toppling through and landed on the floor face-first.

A large wooden chest had been set on the table directly in front of them. As Arty untangled himself and got back to his feet, Emmie creaked open the lid. What would she find? Gold? Jewels? A small monkey wearing a hat?

Nah, it was none of them. It was a small envelope.

"It's a small envelope," said Emmie, who was very observant like that.

"Well, open it, then!" urged Arty. He hopped excitedly from foot to foot, which made the whole tree sway gently back and forth like a metronome.

Emmie tore open the envelope. Maybe there was cash inside. Or a check. Or a very small monkey wearing a hat.

But no.

"It's an invitation to my birthday party tomorrow night!" whooped Arty. "At the town observatory."

"At the what now?" asked Sam.

"The observatory!" said Arty. "It'll be the most informative birthday party you've ever been to. Forget games—we're going to learn all about the wonders of the universe!"

"*Informative*," said Sam.

"*Learning*," said Emmie.

"Yay," they said together.

Arty put his arms around them both, completely failing to notice the sarcasm dripping from their responses. "What's even better is my mom has booked the whole place just for us. We'll have it all to ourselves for hours!"

"Hours?" groaned Emmie.

"Hours!" Arty grinned. "Now, come on," he said. "If we're quick, we can squeeze in one more treasure hunt after lunch!"

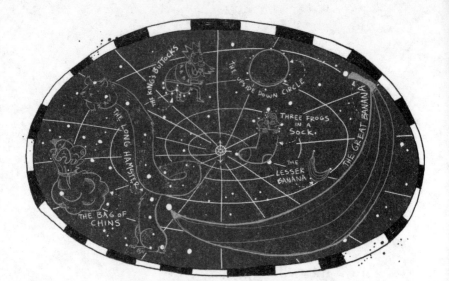

Constellation Spotting

The King's Buttocks

Three Frogs in a Sock

The Great Banana

The Lesser Banana

The Bag of Chins

The Long Hamster

The Upside-Down Circle

CHAPTER TWO

Several long tortuous hours of treasure hunting and an all too brief night's sleep later, Sam, Emmie, and Arty were plonked behind their desks in a biology lesson.

Miss Tribbler had been drafted to replace Professor Pamplemousse following his unfortunate encounter with the zombies. She had been hired by the school three months ago but still seemed to be in a constant state of panic, as if an undead Pamplemousse were going to come shambling through the door at any minute and demand his old job back.

The trouble with Tribbler was that she was a spitter. She didn't do it on purpose, probably.

She'd just get carried away talking about—I don't know—feet or something, and she'd end up spraying blobby bubbles of saliva all over the place. Everyone at the front of the class had taken to wearing raincoats to protect them from the spray, and Miss Tribbler had quickly earned the nickname "Tribbler the Dribbler," which is both rhyming *and* clever, and I dare anyone to say different.

"Think of our humble planet as the most incredible life support machine in the galaxy," she gushed, forcing everyone in the front row to put up their hoods. "It gives us everything: sunlight, water, oxygen. Everything we need to sustain life!"

"Doesn't the Sun give us sunlight?" Emmie asked.

The Dribbler frowned. "Sorry?"

"She's right," Arty said. "Sunlight definitely comes from the Sun. The clue's in the name."

Miss Tribbler began to wring her hands anxiously. This was the cue for everyone at the front to pop up their umbrellas.

"Well . . . y-yes," she said, stammering and spitting in equal measure. "B-but the point I was trying to make was that those things, when taken together, are v-vital to sustain life."

"No amount of sunlight would've sustained Professor Pamplemousse's life," Sam pointed out.

At the merest mention of the old teacher's name, Miss Tribbler's whole body went stiff. Her eyes darted up, down, left, right. She stared at the door for a moment, and then darted across to the windows to check they were shut tight.

"I'd rather we didn't talk about that," she

squeaked at last. She turned back to the blackboard, which wasn't even a blackboard anymore, because they've all been done away with these days, haven't they? It was one of those interactive board things with the buttons and whatnot, but calling it a blackboard is quicker, so let's stick with that.

Her hand shook as she picked up the chalk (in reality a state-of-the-art light pen thingy) and began to write in a trembling and uninteresting sort of a way.

Arty, being very clever, already knew everything Miss Tribbler was teaching in that lesson; Sam, unable to sit still for a minute, wasn't listening anyway.

"So, my party tonight," Arty whispered. "Still coming?"

"Is it still at the observatory?" asked Emmie.

"Yep!"

"Then I can't," Emmie said. "I'm . . . brushing my teeth."

"What, all night?"

Emmie hesitated. "I've got a lot of teeth," she said.

"She's kidding," Sam said. "She'll be there. Won't you?"

With a sigh, Emmie nodded. "Yeah, I'll be there."

Arty almost cheered. "Good," he said. "Because it's going to be *out of this world*!"

He stared at them expectantly.

"Out of this world. We're going to the observatory."

They looked at him blankly.

"With the telescopes and that," Arty continued. "*Out of this world*. Get it?"

Miss Tribbler
Character Profile

1. Overactive saliva glands earned her the nickname Tribbler the Dribbler.

2. Trembling hands—shaking with fear or with barely contained rage. No one quite knows for sure.

3. Shifty eyes are always scanning for misbehaving students and the terrifying reanimated remains of Professor Pamplemousse.

4. Highly strung voice box—her screeches can shatter glass from twenty paces.

5. Running shoes, because you never know when you'll need to flee screaming for your life.

"Yes," said Sam.

"Got it," agreed Emmie, but neither one of them laughed.

Miss Tribbler turned to look their way, and they all put on their best listening faces until she turned back to the ... ahem ... "blackboard."

"Can I just check," whispered Sam, the second her back was turned. "As well as all the learning and informative content of this party—which I'm sure will be fascinating on any number of levels— there is going to be party food, right?"

"Oh yeah," said Arty, who had a huge soft spot for junk food. His stomach. "There's going to be hot dogs and pizza and cake and all that stuff. And we'll get to stay up really late."

"You think eight o'clock's late," Emmie said. "How late are we talking?"

"After midnight at least," Arty said. "It won't be until then that we get the best view of the distant galaxies."

Sam leaned forward in his seat, suddenly interested despite himself. "What do you mean *distant galaxies*? I thought we'd just be looking at the Moon and stuff."

Arty laughed. The sound made The Dribbler's head whip around, spraying slobber in a wide arc across the room. Like a well-rehearsed military exercise, everyone in the class ducked behind their textbooks.

Once the teacher had gone back to her shaky scribbling, Arty continued.

"You can look at the Moon anytime," he said. "The Sitting Duck Observatory has one of the most powerful telescopes in the world!"

"Why?" asked Emmie. "Where did it get that from?"

"Stella won it in a raffle," Arty explained.

"Who's Stella?" asked Sam.

"Stella Gazey, the chief astronomer. She'll be there at the party pointing out all the exciting stuff."

"What, like the exit?" said Emmie, quietly.

"You'll like her," Arty said. "She's cool. And she's really keen on the idea of making contact with distant worlds and alien civilizations."

Emmie rolled her eyes. "Oh yeah," she snorted. "She sounds *really* cool."

It was about then that Sam realized someone was talking to him. It took him a moment to retune his hearing, but then . . .

". . . tell us the answer, Mr. Saunders?"

Sam looked up to find Miss Tribbler staring expectantly at him. She was giving him that evil eye that all teachers get programmed with when they're being put together at the factory.

"Well?" she demanded.

Sam glanced around at the rest of the class, but they all had their hoods and umbrellas up, and he couldn't read anything on their faces.

"Sorry," he said. "Can you repeat the question?"

"Maybe if you would listen once in a while!" the teacher sniped. "I asked you what substance makes up twenty percent of the Earth's atmosphere?"

Sam had absolutely no idea. He puffed out his cheeks and decided to hazard a wild guess. "Jam?"

Ouch. Even I didn't expect it to be quite *that* wild a guess.

"Of course it isn't jam!" spat The Dribbler. "What sort of mess would we all be in if one-fifth of the atmosphere was made of jam?"

"Quite a sticky mess?" Sam ventured.

"Oxygen is the answer, Mr. Saunders," Miss Tribbler sprayed. "Oxygen. Perhaps if you paid more attention you might know the correct answer once in a while. If you want to pass this subject, then I suggest you—"

"Professor Pamplemousse, you're back!" cried Emmie, pointing to the door.

With a scream, Miss Tribbler raced to the stationery cabinet at the back of the classroom and tried to hide inside. Unfortunately, she neglected to open the door. She clattered into it with a *thud*, staggered slightly, then toppled backward onto the floor.

"Oops, sorry," said Emmie, flashing Sam a grin. "False alarm!"

Avoiding a Teacher's Question

So you haven't been paying attention, and now your teacher is going to ask a question and you have absolutely no idea what the answer is. Here are ten handy tips to help you avoid being selected.

1. Don't come in that day.

2. Hide under your desk.

3. Turn invisible.

4. Hide under your desk and turn invisible (better safe than sorry).

5. Move to England. Unless you live in England, in which case move somewhere else.

6. Stick your hand up, wave frantically, and go "Me! Me! Me!" like you can't wait to answer.

7. On second thought, forget #6.

8. Disguise yourself as a lion.

9. Play dead.

10. Come back from the dead. (No one likes a zombie.)

CHAPTER THREE

Arty's mom's car swept up the long gravel driveway leading to the observatory, its headlights cutting through the dark like car headlights through the dark.

Squished between Sam and Arty in the back, Emmie filled everyone in on her latest daring escape. For reasons far too terrible to go into right now, Emmie lives with her Great Aunt Doris. Despite the name, Doris isn't a *great* aunt at all; she's a terrible one. She's always shouting all over the place and trying to make Emmie trim her toenails (Doris's toenails, I mean, not her own) and grounding her for months on end for no reason whatsoever.

Emmie doesn't really pay attention to the shouting, though, and she never goes near the mad old bat's toenails. As for the groundings, Emmie has become a master of escaping right out from under Doris's wrinkled red nose.

"Once I had found the trip wire it was easy," Emmie told them. "I just limboed under the laser beams, tightrope-walked across the washing line, then stuck a bucket over the cat. Same old, same old, really."

"Well, I'm just glad you could make it," Arty said. The car turned a bend and they all slid left. "It's going to be great."

"No, it's going to be *out of this world!*" said Deepta, Arty's mom.

"Ha! Good one, Mrs. Dorkins," said Sam.

"*Out of this world.* Brilliant," agreed Emmie.

"Oh yeah, you laugh when she says it," Arty sulked.

Emmie shrugged. "She tells it better."

"Yeah, she really nailed the delivery," Sam agreed.

They weren't kidding—Deepta really had told the joke better than Arty had, but that wasn't the real reason they laughed along with it. The real reason was that Deepta was Arty's mom, and one of the three unwritten Rules of Friendship is that you should always be polite to your friends' moms. It's the second most important rule, coming before "Friends don't sell friends at auction," and immediately after "Everyone just play nice."

With a screeching of brakes, Deepta brought the car to a screamer of a stop. Arty, Sam, and Emmie were thrown forward in their seats until their seat belts went tight and slammed them back again.

"Nice driving," said Sam.

"Let's get out of here before this maniac kills us all," Emmie mumbled, ignoring the Rules of Friendship completely. She leaned past Sam and threw open the door.

They spilled out onto the gravel drive and there, right before them, like a big overturned bowl with a giant telescope poking out of it, stood the observatory.

"Have fun, you three!" called Arty's mom, then she floored the accelerator and the car sped off down the hill again, back toward the bright lights of Sitting Duck.

"Are you sure the party's tonight?" Sam asked as they made for the front door of the observatory. The entire building was in darkness, with not a light burning in any of the windows. "It looks pretty . . . closed."

"It's definitely tonight," Arty assured him. "I

calculated which day this week would give us optimum visibility of the night sky, and tonight's the night!"

Sam and Emmie peered upward. A cushion of cloud blocked out every one of the stars. "You might want to double-check your calculations," Emmie suggested.

Arty checked his watch and grinned. "Come on, I *always* double-check my calculations," he said. "Three, two, one . . ."

Like a theater curtain, the clouds parted. The sky hung there like a black cloth with a million tiny pinpricks letting light through from the other side. Arty drew in a deep breath and gazed at the wonders of the Universe.

"Pretty impressive, eh?" he said.

"Not bad," Sam admitted.

"Where are these hot dogs, then?" asked Emmie, not all that excited about the wonders of the Universe. Not when there was grub on the go. "I'm starving over here."

With a final glance at the stars, Arty opened the door of the observatory and stepped inside. A still and gloomy silence met them.

"Absolutely certain it's tonight?" said Sam.

"Yeah," said Arty, although he didn't sound all that confident. "I'm . . . I think so." He fumbled about on the wall searching for the light switch until . . .

"Surprise!"

On came the lights, and out of the darkness ran a tall, spindly woman with bulbous, insectlike eyes. Emmie's initial reaction was to punch her to the ground, but luckily she managed to stop herself just in the nick of time.

The woman stopped charging and grinned at them all. The lenses of her round glasses were ridiculously thick. They made her eyes look three or four times bigger than they should be, and Sam wondered if she hadn't gotten her specs mixed up with a couple of telescopes when putting them on that morning.

"Surprise!" the woman said again.

"What is?" asked Sam.

"Er . . . this. The party!"

"No, it isn't," said Emmie.

The woman frowned. "I'm pretty sure it is."

"Does anyone here look surprised?" Emmie asked. She met the woman's wide-eyed stare. "Apart from you, I mean."

The woman dug a skinny hand inside the pocket of her woolly fleece and took out a scrap of paper. She read it quickly, then stuffed it back into the pocket.

"Not surprise!" she chirped. "Definitely not a surprise. Thinking of someone else. Sorry!" She shook their hands one by one, nodding and grinning with each pump of her arm. "Hello! Good evening! I'm Stella. Which one of you is the birthday boy?"

Arty's hand shot up. "Me!"

"Super! Splendid! Many happy, et cetera, et cetera," she said, beaming. "I hope you're ready for a party that's . . . wait for it . . . *out of this world*!" She winked one enormous eye at them. "See what I did there?"

Emmie turned to Sam. "Is it time to go home yet?"

"Ha ha!" whooped Stella. "Don't fret. You've got hours to go before the fun's over! What should we do first?"

"Eat cake," suggested Emmie.

"Watch television?" suggested Sam.

"*Buzz!* Wrong answers," laughed Stella, quietly congratulating herself for throwing in a fleeting reference to Buzz Aldrin, the second man to set foot on the surface of the Moon. Which she knew all about, obviously, because that sort of stuff is right up her alley. "We don't even have a television up here."

Sam gestured to the banks of screens that took up one whole wall of the room. "What about them?"

"Those aren't televisions—they're computer screens," Stella said. She flicked one on and rows and rows of bright green numbers scrolled across the display.

"What does all that mean?" asked Emmie.

"I have absolutely no idea," Stella confessed. "Sometimes they're green. Occasionally they go orange. Every once in a while it makes a sort of bleeping noise. I tend not to bother with it, really. I'm much more interested in"—she turned their attention to a bank of dials and switches on the opposite side of the room—"this."

Sam, Arty, and Emmie approached the

equipment. Static hissed from a large wooden speaker, broken every so often by a high-pitched chirp.

"Is that what I think it is?" asked Arty in a hushed whisper.

"Do you think it's a state-of-the-art radio transmitting and receiving unit, harvesting waves from all across the known galaxies?"

Arty nodded. "That's exactly what I think it is."

"Then no, it's not one of those," Stella said. Her wide eyes widened even farther, so they took up half her face. "It's a state-of-the-art radio transmitting and receiving unit that's harvesting waves from all the known *and unknown* galaxies!"

"Whoa!" gasped Arty. "So you can use that to listen into signals from outer space?"

"From other worlds!" cried Stella. "Eventually," she added. "If we ever find one."

Emmie leaned closer to Sam. "What a waste," she whispered. "If I had that, I'd be listening in to everyone in Sitting Duck all day. You'd be able to hear them all gossiping and arguing and . . ."

"Farting."

Emmie winced. "Oh yeah. Didn't think of that."

"Any questions so far?" asked Stella.

"Yeah," replied Emmie. "Any chance of something to eat?"

"Yes! Yes! Very soon," said Stella, clapping her hands excitedly. "But first . . . I wonder if anyone here would like a look at my telescope?"

"Not particularly," shrugged Emmie.

"If we must," said Sam.

"Ooh, me! Me!" yelped Arty.

"Then onward!" announced Stella, marching toward a set of double doors at the back of the room. Arty raced to keep up, leaving Sam and Emmie trailing along behind. They glanced at each other and sighed. There was no doubt about it.

It was going to be a very long night.

☆ ☆ ☆

Other Things That Have Been Spotted by the Telescope in Sitting Duck

- Another much smaller telescope

- Great Aunt Doris hanging out her frilly knickers

- A man carrying a fridge

- Zombies eating people's faces off. I mean, like, *right off*. It was horrible.

- A duck (sadly not sitting)

- Arty's brother, Jesse, shrugging a lot and looking confused

- A really exciting but completely top secret thing

- Some houses

Time passed. To Sam and Emmie, it felt like weeks. To Arty, it felt like just a few minutes. Who's to say which of them was right?

Me, actually. And they were both wrong. It was three hours, nine minutes, and eleven seconds.

Arty had spent the most fascinating evening of his young life gazing up at the heavens, admiring the stars and ignoring the Moon, because what's the point of looking at that when you can see it pretty much any night you want, and even in the daytime sometimes when it's getting ideas above its station?

Sam and Emmie had eaten pizza and hot dogs and planet-shaped fizzy sweets until they felt sick. It was after 11 PM now, and although the sugar surging through their veins meant they weren't tired, they both wanted to go home.

"Guys!" cried Arty, peering through the viewfinder of the telescope exactly like he had been for the past hour and a half. "You won't believe what I'm seeing!"

"Is it another big lump of rock?" Emmie guessed.

"It's a meteor!" Arty yelped.

"Which, when you think about it, is another way of saying a big lump of rock," Sam said.

Arty was about to reply

when the clanging of an alarm echoed around the room. Emmie and Sam bounded to their feet.

"What does that mean?" asked Emmie hopefully. "Is it home-time?"

Stella frowned. She raced over to another bank of monitors and hurriedly clicked on the screens. "I'm . . . I'm not sure," she said.

The letters on the screens came into view. They were red and flashing furiously.

"Are they supposed to be doing that?" Sam asked, shouting to make himself heard over the din.

"Again, not sure," Stella admitted. "Never seen it do that before!"

On the far side of the room a printer began vomiting out reams of paper. Stella darted over, and as she read the printout her eyes became wide enough to eat your dinner off.

"Arty, turn that telescope!" she cried. "Eighteen degrees west, twenty-seven degrees north."

Arty didn't need telling twice. He spun a little handle down near the lens of the telescope and the whole thing began to swivel into position. Locking it in place, Arty pressed his eye up against the viewfinder.

He leaned back.

He blinked.

He leaned in again.

"Uh, guys . . ."

"Let me guess," said Emmie. "More rocks?"

Arty looked up. "N-no," he said. "It's a . . . It's a . . ."

"It's a what?" shrieked Stella.

Arty chewed his bottom lip nervously. "It's a UFO!"

Space Jokes!

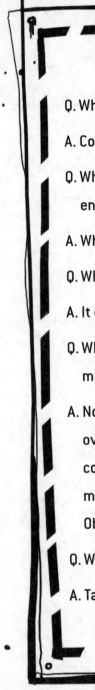

Q. What do aliens like to read?

A. Comet books!

Q. When does the Moon know it has had enough to eat?

A. When it's full!

Q. Why did the cow go into outer space?

A. It didn't. NASA sent a mouse instead.

Q. Which of the planets is the only one to be married?

A. None of them. Planets were formed over millions of years as matter was condensed into spinning spheres of molten mass. They can't get married. Obviously.

Q. What did the alien say to the garden?

A. Take me to your weeder!

CHAPTER FOUR

"Very funny," tutted Emmie. "Stop trying to make this interesting. It's not going to work."

"I'm serious!" Arty cried.

"Yeah, right," said Sam.

Stella bounced excitedly from foot to foot. "This is it!" she yelped. "This is it! After all these years! Let's have a look."

She flicked a number of important-looking switches and pointed to one of the monitors. "Behold!"

Nothing happened.

"Any minute . . . now!" she said.

Nothing happened.

"Now!" Stella said. "Wait for it . . . now!"

"Does it need to be plugged in?" asked Sam, holding up a power cord.

Stella gave an embarrassed cough. "Um . . . go on, then."

Sam plugged in the monitor and suddenly everyone could see what Arty was seeing through the telescope.

Emmie got slowly to her feet. "It's . . . It's . . ."

Sam stared. Arty stared. Stella came dangerously close to wetting herself with excitement. Even Emmie held back on the wisecracks, which really wasn't like her at all. Everyone expected her to come out with something sarcastic as usual, but instead she just said: "What *is* that?"

"A flying saucer," breathed Arty, and he wasn't far off. The thing buzzing around in front of the

Moon was definitely saucer-shaped, only bigger, obviously, because saucers are far too small to go winging around in space all by themselves.

The saucer seemed to shudder as it moved back and forth, back and forth in front of the Moon's big Moon face. It reminded Sam of the spaceship from a fuzzy old black-and-white sci-fi film he had watched late one night when he couldn't sleep. If he had to give the UFO a score for special effects, it'd be a three at most, and he still couldn't quite believe that what he was seeing was real.

"Is this real?" he asked, right on cue. "Or are you winding us up?"

"I assure you it's absolutely positively happening!" yelped Stella. "We're witnessing an actual real-life unidentified flying object!"

"Uh, guys . . ." said Arty.

"Yes, very funny," sighed Emmie. "Joke's over now, though. We're not falling for it."

"Guys!"

"You had us going for a minute, though," Sam admitted. "So, you know, well done, but—"

"GUYS!"

Arty's voice echoed around the observatory. He pointed at the monitor and everyone turned to look.

"Am I seeing things," he began, "or is it getting bigger?"

The object wasn't growing larger in the sky; it was getting closer. Quite quickly, in fact. Actually, really very quickly indeed. It seemed to race directly toward the telescope, the silver saucerlike chassis spinning as it closed the gap between the Moon and the Earth.

There was a bright green flash as the spacecraft punched through the planet's atmosphere. It was almost filling the view-screen now, all sleek and silver with a big domed window on top.

It became a blur across the monitor as the telescope struggled to maintain its focus, just like I sometimes have difficulty in . . . Oooh, a butterfly. How nice.

And then the spaceship was gone. Darkness

 filled the screen again, dotted here and there with distant shimmering stars.

"What happened?" asked Sam. "Where did it go?"

A screaming noise from overhead made them all duck. It made the room rumble as it swooshed by. Sam was up and racing to the window much more quickly than I would've done, because I'm instinctively a coward by nature.

The others joined him as he gazed out onto the most amazing scene he'd ever seen. The flying saucer was hovering directly above Sitting Duck. It hung there in the air exactly like a brick wouldn't, lights blinking along its aluminum skin, the streetlamps below reflecting off its patterns of polished chrome.

Although the UFO wasn't moving, it spun
constantly like a spinning top powered by magic.
As it rotated, it emitted a high-pitched whistling
noise, which was probably torture for all the dogs
in the area, but no one thought to ask them.

"Well," said Sam, under his breath. "There's
something you don't see every day."

"No one's seen it before!" breathed Stella.
"Don't you see? We're the first people to ever
witness this. We've just discovered alien life!"

"Go us!" said Emmie.

"Are they friendly?" asked Arty.

"Oh, I should think so," said Stella, waving a
hand. "Bound to be. Yes. Bound to be."

With a series of clicks, every monitor in the
observatory switched on. Even those not plugged
in blinked into life with the rest of them. For a

moment, nothing seemed to happen, but then numbers started to shimmy across the screen one after another like a big conga line, but with numbers. And no music.

Sam squinted at the digits dashing by on the screen. "What's this?" he wondered. He looked down to see numbers flashing across:

20.1.11.5 13.5 20.15

25.15.21.18 12.5.1.4.5.18

"What does it mean?" asked Emmie.

"It's a code!" cried Arty.

Sam and Emmie groaned. "Not another one."

"Of course!" cried Stella. "The computer is translating the message from the aliens into numerical code, because numbers are universal! Mathematical constants are mathematical constants regardless of where you are in the Universe!"

Emmie let out a loud snore. "Sorry, nodded off there," she said. "What does any of that mean?"

"It means the numbers represent letters, just like in my code-breaking kit," Arty said.

Arty grabbed a pencil and began to scribble. His hand became a blur of speed as he frantically tried to translate the coded message on screen.

"Got it!" he said, surprisingly quickly, all things considered. "I've worked out the message."

"Well?" demanded Emmie.

"Grmg ft ak hrou pedkar," Arty said.

Everyone blinked in surprise.

"Eh?" said Stella.

"You sure?" asked Sam.

Arty nodded. "Yeah, think so. Unless . . ." He

turned the page upside down, squinted, then did a bit more scribbling. "Ah no, my mistake," he said, blushing slightly. "It says, 'Take me to your leader.'"

Emmie rolled her eyes. "That's the single most unoriginal thing any alien could ever say," she said. "I can't believe they traveled millions of miles and that was the best they could come up with."

Sam pointed to the radio broadcasting equipment they'd only just been looking at in the previous chapter. "Can we use that to send them a message back?"

"Yes!" yelped Stella, and for a moment Sam thought her head might actually explode with excitement. "We can! We can send them a message!"

"What will we say?" asked Arty.

"Tell them we're not in," suggested Emmie.

"No," said Sam. "Tell them we'll be happy to bring them to our leader. Tell them to meet us at the Town Hall."

He yawned and stretched. "But tell them it'll have to wait until tomorrow. I don't know about you guys, but I *really* need to get some sleep."

Know Your UFOs

Something that Stella might have found useful is the very popular book that I've just this minute written called *The A–Z of UFOs and Stuff* by R. McGeddon—available now from me at my house. Here are just a few sample entries for your information and enjoyment.

A is for Alpha Centauri Shuttle Bus: Large, cumbersome, and a blinding shade of bright yellow, this spacecraft is best known for carrying retirees from their home in the Alpha Centauri galaxy to the bingo hall just along the road.

F is for Flipping Fast: Most UFOs (with the exception of the Alpha Centauri Shuttle Bus) rattle along at a right old pace. Imagine the fastest fighter jet ever invented on Earth. Then double it. Then double it again. Then take a tiny bit away. That's *the slowest speed they can go*! Probably.

P is for Packed with Stuff: From aliens to star maps to fancy gadgets that go *blooop*, UFOs are crammed full of stuff. You'd think this would make them heavier, but thanks to amazing outer space technology it actually makes them lighter. No one really knows why.

T is for Trans-Galactic Express: Need to get from Globblewhitz 9 in the Rohandor system to Pimfizzle Minor on the outer rim in a hurry? The Trans-Galactic Express will get you there in just under thirty Earth minutes. Granted, the crushing g-forces will turn your bones to a soft paste before you're past Globblewhitz 8, but when time is of the essence, the TGE is the way to travel.

X is for Xit: Because despite their advanced technologies and vast knowledge, aliens just cannot manage to spell *exit* correctly.

CHAPTER FIVE

What with the alien spaceship being really
massive and hovering over the town making
a whistling noise, it did not go unnoticed by
the good people of Sitting Duck. They weren't the
most observant folks in the world, but even they
could spot an enormous silver saucer that more or
less blocked out the sky.

Stella had spread the word about the message
the aliens had sent, and bright and early the next
morning everyone had gathered at the Town Hall,
desperate to be among the first to see what these
strangers from outer space looked like.

Say what you like about the Sitting Duckers,
they're nothing if not polite. Many of them had

brought balloons and little flags with them. Some had made cakes and cookies, and little cardboard signs with "We Heart Aliens" on them, only the heart was a drawing of a love-heart done in jumbo crayon with glitter around it.

Make no mistake about it, they were all on the excited side, and the flashing of cameras and

chatter of TV news anchors only made them worse.

Sam, Emmie, and Arty moved through the packed crowd with ease. Everyone knew not to get in Emmie's way if they wanted to avoid a boot to the shins, and the throngs seemed to part whenever she approached.

On a raised platform right outside the Town Hall stood Mayor Sozzle.

Actually *stood* is a bit on the generous side. He sort of slumped there, an arm around one of his officials, looking a bit out of sorts.

"Issamazin'," he slurred, raising a hand to the flying saucer as if saluting. "Issamazin' big shasepip." He frowned. "Spapeshish."

The official slapped him hard across the face.

"Spaceship," the mayor managed. He gave his aide a nod. "Thanks."

"My pleasure," said the official, and it was, because he really disliked the mayor, and slapping him hard across the face was the only thing that made his job worthwhile. Which is understandable given the mayor's last aide was eaten by a zombie.

Dos and Don'ts When Greeting Alien Visitors

- **Do** stand up straight.

- **Don't** wear stilts.

- **Do** be polite and courteous.

- **Don't** kiss them on the lips.

- **Do** extend a welcome on behalf of the planet Earth.

- **Don't** tell them they look like that weird kid from your math class.

- **Do** ask how their journey was.

- **Don't** scream "You've come to take me home!" at the top of your voice, then run into their spaceship laughing.

Emmie led Sam and Arty to the front of the crowd. Arty groaned when he realized his older brother, Jesse, was already there. Jesse's nostrils flared when he spotted them, as if he'd just smelled something deeply unpleasant.

"Well, well, well." He scowled. "If it isn't the Three Muskadweebs."

"Incredible!" said Arty. "You've finally learned to count to three. Mom and Dad are going to be so proud."

"Shut it, loser," Jesse growled. He pointed up to the saucer hovering above them. "Your ride's here."

"What's that supposed to mean?" asked Arty.

"I've always said you were some weird alien life-form," Jesse sneered. "They've come to take you home." He turned to Sam and Emmie. "Enjoy his dorky birthday party, did you?"

"Yeah, it was brilliant, actually," said Sam.

"Loved every minute," agreed Emmie.

"Maybe you should go hide somewhere, though," Sam suggested.

Jesse frowned. "What? Why?"

"Well, the aliens have come all this way to find intelligent life. If they see you, they'll probably turn around and go home again."

Jesse wasn't the sharpest tool in the shed, and so it took him a full thirty seconds to realize Sam had insulted him, and a good ten seconds more to decide what he was going to do about it.

Just as he had decided what he was going to do—which involved a hedge, three baseballs, and a glass slipper—he was distracted by an arm slipping around his. They all turned to see a blond-haired girl with a furry pink coat

fluttering her false eyelashes
Jesse's way.

"Hey, boyfriend,"
she said. "Hey . . .
you three."

"Hi, Phoebe,"
said Sam,
without much
enthusiasm.
Arty gave the
girl a brief
wave. Emmie

crammed her fist in her mouth and did her best
not to scream.

Phoebe, it was safe to say, was not one of Emmie's
all-time top ten favorite people. She wasn't even
in her top hundred. In fact, Emmie wasn't entirely

sure she even qualified as a person. She was more like an annoying itch you couldn't scratch that refused to go away, only with lots of money and designer clothes and a way of talking that made Emmie want to gouge her own ears out with a spoon. Not for the first time, Emmie wished they'd left Phoebe as a zombie when they'd had the chance.

"Like, this is totes crazy," said Phoebe. Emmie gnawed on her knuckles and resisted the urge to wring Phoebe's neck. "How bling is that big spinny dish? Like OMG!"

"I'm not your boyfriend," Jesse said. "Why do you keep following me?"

Phoebe let out a shrill laugh and squeezed Jesse's arm. "He is such a kidder! You are such a kidder! That's why we make such a totally perfect couple! He's so funny, I'm . . ."

"Evil in a dress?" Emmie muttered. "The most irritating human being alive?"

"Well, *gorgeous* is what I was going to say, if you must know," Phoebe said. She sniffed and looked down her nose at Emmie and the others. "So, like, this big OUF or whatever they're calling it. I heard from this guy, who heard from this guy, who heard from these other guys, who read something on like, wherever, that you three spotted it first. Is that true?"

"It most certainly is," said Arty proudly.

"Then I'm, like, totally staying away from it," Phoebe said. "Anytime I get involved with you three it's, like, OMG—Disaster City."

Sam looked offended. "How can you say that?"

"Hello?" Phoebe trilled. "Last time we hung out I got turned into a zombie."

"Not for long, though," Sam reminded her. "It can't have been that bad."

"I ate an old lady!"

"Yeah, I suppose that *is* pretty bad," Sam admitted.

"Anyway, their big saucer thing has full-scale ruined my phone signal. I've been in a social media blackout since it arrived." She held up her phone. "There could be things happening out there in the world right now that I have no idea about, all because of this big chunk of stupid."

"Don't worry, Jesse," said Sam. "She didn't mean you."

Before Jesse could reply, a gasp went up from the crowd. Sam and the others turned in time to see a bright red beam descend from the bottom of the spaceship. Looking directly into the light made their eyes ache, but there was no way they were going to look away. Not now. Not when three figures were gliding gracefully down inside the beam and alighting on the street outside the Town Hall.

The light vanished, leaving the three figures behind. The aliens looked at the people of Sitting Duck. The people of Sitting Duck looked at the aliens.

"They're smaller than I expected," whispered Arty, and Sam nodded in agreement.

The aliens were tiny. Their bodies were short and squat, and their square heads barely came up to knee-height of the surrounding adults. Their teeny-tiny features were scrunched up near the bottom of their heads, like a cute wittle baby's, and their skin was nearly as lumpy as school cafeteria custard, but not the same color. It was blue. As they turned and cast their gazes across the gathered crowds, their silver space suits rustled faintly.

Up on stage the mayor grinned happily. He tried to speak, but a sudden fit of the hiccups prevented him from delivering the heartfelt welcome address he'd scribbled on the back of a coaster over breakfast.

All around Sam and the others, the Sitting Duckers were smiling and waving at the aliens. Many of them had their phones out to record this historic event for future generations to ignore on the

Internet, because they'll all be watching funny videos about cats on skateboards instead. They were acting as if the aliens were old friends returning from a trip abroad, but something about the little blue figures was making Sam uneasy.

At first he wasn't sure what it was. It might have been something in their body language as they approached the mayor, their little legs pumping fast like pistons. It might have been the expressions on their little baby faces or the way their eyes darted left and right as they walked.

But it was probably their ray guns, Sam reckoned. Two of the three aliens carried them— sleek silver weapons about the size of a large zucchini but not nearly as good for your health. Their stubby fingers gripped the triggers as the

leader of their little
group scampered
closer and closer to
the mayor.

"Wahey!"
cheered Mayor
Sozzle, stumbling
down the steps at
the front of the Town
Hall and almost trampling all three of the ETs to
death. "Who's a little cutie-pie, then?" he slurred.
He stooped and snatched up the only unarmed
member of the group and patted it affectionately
on the top of its glass helmet.

"I really don't think he should be doing that,"
mumbled Arty.

"Oh, chill," said Phoebe, forcing Sam to

physically restrain Emmie. "Look at that thing—it's too cute. Seriously, what's the worst that could happen?"

Zzzzzzap!

The two aliens not currently being nuzzled in the mayor's arms opened fire. A crackle of blinding light spat from the barrels. The mayor's hair stood on end.

"Heh. That tickles," he giggled. And then, without any warning whatsoever, he exploded in a glittering shower of sparkles.

"*That*, probably," said Sam, and then the entire crowd began to scream.

Defend Yourself from an Alien Sneak Attack

So aliens have invaded your planet? Bummer. Don't worry, I've put together this list of techniques you might want to put into use should one of those pesky invaders try to kill you in unpleasant ways. Be aware that some of these techniques will only be effective against specific alien races. While it is possible, for example, to tickle a member of the Fluffpuffle race into submission, this strategy will be somewhat less effective against the captain of a Venusian Death Fleet.

- Tie up its tentacles when it isn't looking.

- Shoot it with a ray gun (note: requires ray gun).

- Stuff cotton wool in its gills.

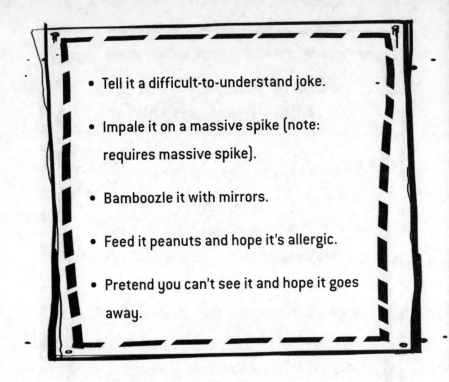

- Tell it a difficult-to-understand joke.

- Impale it on a massive spike (note: requires massive spike).

- Bamboozle it with mirrors.

- Feed it peanuts and hope it's allergic.

- Pretend you can't see it and hope it goes away.

CHAPTER SIX

For all their faults (and there are many), the people of Sitting Duck perform pretty well under pressure. Having come through a zombie apocalypse more or less unscathed—not counting all the ones who died, had legs bitten off, or ate their families—the mayor being vaporized by two tiny men from outer space wasn't all that big a deal, and they stopped screaming almost immediately.

To tell you the truth, they didn't really scream at all. I just wanted to end that last chapter with some screaming, because that's always a nice way to end a chapter, if you ask me. They actually just sort of stared in confusion, but that would've been a terrible chapter ending, don't you think? So let's just pretend they screamed for a little bit, then pulled themselves together quite quickly, okay?

They watched the shimmering cloud of dust, which had until very recently been the mayor, drift away on the breeze; killing a government official with an alien death ray didn't exactly say "We come in peace."

As the mayor became nothing but particles, the alien he was holding fell to the ground. It bounced once on its fishbowl-like helmet, then clambered to its feet with as much dignity as it could muster, which, quite frankly, wasn't much.

The alien leader turned to the crowd, and in what was surely one of those all-time defining moments in history, spoke the first word ever spoken on Earth by a visitor from outer space.

"Buttocks," it said, much to everyone's surprise.

"Did he just say 'buttocks'?" whispered Sam.

"Sounded like it," said Emmie.

"Why would an alien come all this way just to say 'buttocks'?" wondered Arty, but before he could wonder anymore, the alien spoke up again.

"Buttox-traktai-sumalum-paktoo," it squawked. The other two members of his little group nodded in a way that was 50 percent menacing, 50 percent *just too cute.*

A murmur of confusion rippled through the crowd. The alien leader stared at them expectantly, clearly waiting for some sort of response. When it didn't get one, it turned to its companions and hurriedly began to whisper.

With two little hops, the aliens were suddenly

standing one on top of the other to address the
crowd at something approaching eye level. One
of the minions stood on the shoulders of the
other, while the leader balanced on top of him.

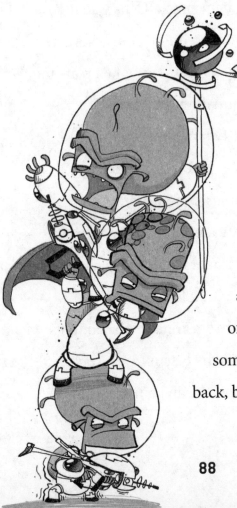

They looked
like a little
blue-and-silver
totem pole.
All around,
the audience's
cameras popped
and flashed.
There was even
a faint smattering
of applause from
somewhere near the
back, but it died off quickly

when the alien leader flicked a switch on his helmet and began to speak. This time no one could fail to understand his message.

"People of Earth," he said in perfect English. His voice was surprisingly gruff for someone so small. It took everyone by surprise, as if a tiny kitten had just started to bark.

"That switch must've activated a translator," said Arty, who'd watched space movies loads of times and knew all about that sort of stuff. Emmie shushed him as the alien continued to speak.

"We came in peace," the alien said, and a cheer of relief went up from the crowd.

"*Came* in peace," the alien said, raising his voice. "Then your leader tried to stroke me like a pet Gagglepuss and we changed our minds."

The crowd stopped cheering.

"I am Quarg, Grand High Ruler of the Baad-Vaart."

"I've been *Baad-Vaarting* all morning," Sam smirked. "I think it was all those hot dogs I ate last night."

"We have traveled across thousands of light-years, drawn by the broadcasts of the Earthling you call Stella Gazey."

All eyes turned to Stella. Her wide eyes blinked rapidly, and she gave a nervous little wave to all the angry faces glaring her way.

"Oh, well, thanks a lot," said more or less everyone at exactly the same time.

"She made it sound like such a nice place we decided we must come and see it for ourselves," Quarg said. "You are extremely fortunate to have such an amazing planet. It teems with life from its deepest oceans to its highest peaks. It boasts sights unmatched in this galactic sector. It offers experiences that inhabitants of other worlds could only dream of."

The crowd mumbled in agreement. The Earth wasn't that bad, actually, when you thought about it.

"And now, it belongs to us," said Quarg. "As of this moment, the planet Earth is under Baad-Vaart control. Do not attempt to resist."

"Oh yeah?" demanded an angry voice from the crowd. "Why, what are you going to do about it if we do?"

"Shoot you in the face," said Quarg.

"Oh," said the voice in the crowd. "Right, yeah. Sorry I asked."

"Any other questions?" asked Quarg. He cast his gaze across the audience. "No? Good. Then let the total domination of the planet begin!"

With a deeply worrying *whumming* noise, several insectlike legs extended from inside the spaceship. The legs touched down onto the street. A series of tiny hatches opened and suddenly the streets were filled with hundreds of the little alien figures. They all wore identical space suits and carried weapons of various shapes and sizes, each one more deadly looking than the last.

Guide to Cool Cosmic Weaponry

Alien weaponry is much better than the junk we've got kicking around here on Earth. I mean . . . *spears*! How boring are they? Aliens have got much better stuff in their cabinets, and here are just a few of them.

THE RAY GUN: There are various types of ray gun available to the gun-toting alien around town today. From those that shoot concentrated blasts of laser fire to those that dissolve targets into their component molecules, there's something to suit every murderous taste.

THE ACCELORAGER: One blast from this highly advanced weapon will take years off your life—literally. An exposure of just one second will age your body by anything up to forty years, giving you a bald head, too many chins, and a worrying amount of hair sprouting from your nostrils.

THE INSANITIZER: Have you ever had a tune stuck in your head that you can't quite place but won't go away? You know how it drove you nuts until you almost wanted to scream? Imagine that feeling a thousand times worse and you're not even close to the effects of the Insanitizer. A single shot from this weapon will make even the most balanced individual implode in a fit of maddening frustration.

It finally occurred to the people of Sitting Duck that they should probably run away. They turned as one like a shoal of fish, but with legs, and began hoofing it off in every direction, fleeing as fast as they could from the blue-skinned spacemen. And probably spacewomen, too, but it's quite hard to tell by looking at them. It's not like any of them had beards or anything.

Laser fire scorched the air and half a dozen fleeing townsfolk became pretty sparkles, and then became nothing at all.

"I *totally* knew this was going to happen," Phoebe snapped. "What did I say? Hang out with you three and this is what happens. First zombies, now aliens. This might sound harsh, but we totally cannot be friends anymore."

"Oh well," shrugged Emmie. "The day isn't a total write-off, then."

"Do not attempt to flee, Earthlings," commanded Quarg. "You cannot escape. Allow me to demonstrate the extent of our power."

There was a brief flash of light from somewhere

within the spaceship, followed by a sound like a
cat being sucked up a vacuum cleaner. Then the
air was filled with smoke and dust and
dirty great lumps of rock as the
Town Hall was blown to
smithereens.

The people of Sitting Duck immediately stopped running. They stood there, side by side, staring in confusion and proving my point that this really isn't a very good way to end a chapter.

CHAPTER SEVEN

Quarg clearly hadn't thought his plan through. Rather than stop the Sitting Duckers from running in terror, blowing up the Town Hall just made them more determined to get away. After the initial shock had passed, they were off like a shot, clambering over fences, scrambling over walls, dashing and darting this way and that as the screams of laser fire filled the air around them.

"Right, cut it out!" Quarg barked. "Stop running away—I'm warning you."

A troop of the tiny aliens advanced on Sam and the others, their little faces scrunched up into an expression halfway between menacing and adorable. They blasted wildly into the crowd, and one of Sam's neighbors lit up like a firework, then fizzled away to nothing.

"This way," Sam urged, ducking behind a chunk of the Town Hall roof just as a laser blast tore past him. Jesse clattered off with Phoebe still hanging onto his arm. Arty and Emmie stuck with Sam as he wove down an alleyway, although why he thought he had time to waste weaving with all these aliens kicking about is anyone's guess.

A scuffing of tiny feet told him that the ETs were giving chase. Sam snatched up a trash-can lid and raised it like a shield. A blast from an alien ray gun deflected off the metal lid and ricocheted into the air, tragically killing an entire family of geese that were flying overhead at the time and minding their own business.

"Nicely done," said Emmie.

"Thanks," said Sam.

There was a series of loud *thuds* as eight crispy-fried geese rained down around them. "Where did they come from?" asked Arty.

"Come on," yelped Emmie, snatching up a lid of her own. "Let's get out of here!"

They raced along the alleyway, ducking and dodging as more laser fire streaked by. At the end of the alley, they spilled out onto Parrot's Walk, darted past the dart shop, and found themselves knee-to-face with a dozen of the little blue creatures.

Emmie and Sam raised their lids in time to deflect the first few energy beams. With a high-pitched squeal that would have been pretty adorable under any other circumstances, one of the aliens hurled itself at Emmie.

She raised the lid and brought it down with a *clang* on the ET's helmet. It staggered for a moment, too dazed to dodge as Emmie drew back her foot and punted it over the heads of its fellow invaders.

"Arty, look out!" cried Sam, as another of the aliens opened fire. With a flick of his wrist, Sam hurled his trash-can lid. It sliced toward his friend, and Arty snatched it from the air just as the energy beam reached him.

The blast bounced off the makeshift shield, back the way it had come. The alien gunman's eyes went wide and it gave a little whimper, before exploding in a shower of glittery sparks.

The aliens hesitated. It was just for a moment, but it was long enough for Sam and Emmie to throw themselves over a wall, dragging Arty along behind them. They heard the aliens chitter angrily, but they were too small to follow, and by the time they had hopped up onto one another's shoulders, Sam and the others had vanished.

"It's not safe out on the streets," Sam

whispered. They were pressed up together behind a small garden shed, watching the invaders scuttle off in search of someone else to shoot at.

"Oh, you think so?" said Emmie. "What gave you that idea?"

"The aliens and stuff," said Sam, who had never really gotten the hang of sarcasm. "Let's go to my house. We'll be safe there."

"How come we always go to your house when we're running for our lives?" asked Emmie. "Why do we never go to my house?"

Sam shrugged. "We can if you want. You probably want to check on Doris, I'd imagine."

Emmie flinched. "Let's go to your house," she said. "We'll be safe there."

"I hope Jesse hasn't been vaporized," Arty said.

Sam rested a hand on his friend's shoulder. "Don't worry. He'll be fine."

"Oh, I'm not worried," Arty said. "It's just that if he's going to be blown to bits I'd like to see it, is all."

"Er . . . right," said Sam.

"In slow motion, ideally."

"You have a deeply unhealthy relationship with your brother," Sam told him. From somewhere nearby they heard the chattering of more aliens. "Now come on, let's get out of here while we still can."

☆ ☆ ☆

Full-Scale Alien Defense Plans

You've just had a message from the scientists back at HQ—an alien armada has been spotted zooming past Mars. It's going to be here any minute! While your initial urge might be to run around screaming "We're all going to die!" try not to panic yet—there may still be time to initiate your planetwide defense plan.

You do have a planetwide defense plan, right? If not, feel free to borrow one of mine from below.

PLAN A: Shoot Them with Nuclear Missiles. One missile alone won't be enough, so best to fire them all to be on the safe side. The resulting explosion might well take out the

Moon, but what has the Moon ever done for us? Given us werewolves, that's what. Good riddance, I say.

PLAN B: Hide. Using some sort of pulley system and a really long stick, we hide the entire planet behind Uranus. No one will ever think to look there.

PLAN C: Set Up an Out-of-Planet Automatic Responder. When the aliens attempt to make contact, the automatic responder will tell them we're not in and won't be back until the year 2150. This will buy us more time to think of another plan.

PLAN D: Pretend to Surrender, Then Run Away When They Aren't Looking. Pretty self-explanatory, really.

ALIENS!

It took the friends ages to make their way to Sam's house, what with all the death and destruction and people running about screaming and stuff. When they finally barged in through the back door, they almost crashed straight into Sam's dad.

"Hey-ho," he said to them, although he wasn't sure why. He'd never said "hey-ho" before, and he was quite surprised to find himself saying it now. He'd never thought of himself as a "hey-ho" sort of person.

From somewhere behind him there was a loud

ping of advanced technology. Sam hurled himself on top of his dad, pulling him to the kitchen floor.

"Down!" Sam yelped. "Stay down!"

"Um . . . why?" asked his dad, although his voice was muffled somewhat by Sam lying across his head. "I'll miss the film. Incidentally," he added, "I can't breathe."

Sam sat back. "Film? What film?"

"It's a science fiction thing," his dad said. "It's very realistic. I was just getting some popcorn for me and your mom."

Sam looked up at the microwave and realized that that was what had made the pinging sound he had heard. He got to his feet and helped his dad up. Emmie and Arty followed them as Sam's dad grabbed the popcorn and headed through to the front room.

"Hurry up with that popcorn," urged Sam's mom. She was sitting on the couch with a cushion on her lap, watching aliens shoot the place up on TV. "This is getting good. They just blew up the Town Hall."

"Oh, did they?" groaned Sam's dad. "I'd have loved to have seen that."

"Amazing special effects," said Sam's mom. She turned to Sam. "I say, it's amazing special effects. So realistic!"

Arty cleared his throat. "Actually, Mrs. Saunders . . ."

A look from Sam silenced him.

"Yes, dear?"

"Er . . . I was just going to say that, um . . ."

"That this film won an award for its special effects," said Emmie.

"I'm not surprised," said Sam's dad. "One of the little alien fellas shot the mayor a while back and *whoosh!* Gone. You could almost smell the burning, couldn't you, love?"

"You could," agreed Sam's mom. "You could almost smell the burning."

A panic-stricken woman with dark hair and a darker suit appeared on-screen holding a microphone. The footage flickered and the woman's audio spat and crackled and hissed in and out.

"... full scale invasion ... Baad-Vaart ... dozens dead ..."

"Oh, what's she in?" asked Sam's mom. "I've seen her somewhere before. What was it now?"

"The news?" Sam suggested.

"No, no, she's an actress, isn't she? She was in

one of them hospital things or something. Oh, what was it?"

While his mom tried to figure out what the news reporter had been in before, Sam turned his attention to the TV. The woman was no longer on the screen. Instead, the footage was coming from a camera mounted on a helicopter somewhere a few miles outside Sitting Duck.

Sam, Emmie, and Arty stared as a

flickering dome of purple energy fizzled into life above the town. It sat there like a huge upturned bowl—a bit like the observatory, but without the massive telescope poking out the top.

The picture changed, and suddenly the huge eyes of Stella Gazey filled the screen, with a cameo appearance from the rest of her face.

"Hey, it's Stella," said Sam. "What's she doing on the news?"

The sound continued to crackle in and out, but Stella's message was still easy enough to understand.

". . . sort of energy barrier . . . any attempts to leave or enter Sitting Duck are proving deadly . . . people being fried to a crisp on contact . . . to leave . . . repeat, do not attempt to leave."

"What is she, official alien spokesperson now?" Emmie wondered.

"They're barricading us in," Arty realized. "It's a force field. No one gets in and no one gets out. They've trapped everyone. It's only a matter of time before they wipe out everyone in town."

"Gosh," said Sam's dad, scooping up a handful of popcorn and stuffing it into his mouth. "Isn't that an exciting twist?"

CHAPTER EIGHT

Days passed and the town of Sitting Duck went back to normal. Except, actually, it didn't. It turned out the aliens didn't want to kill everyone in town after all, which was nice. They wanted to enslave them instead. Which wasn't very nice.

The shops were still open, although the shopkeepers were all now aliens. The police still did their rounds although, now that I think about it, they had been replaced by aliens, too. It was pretty much aliens wherever you looked actually, and the school was no exception.

Sam, Emmie, Arty, and all the other students sat in the science class listening to the teacher. Tribbler the Dribbler had been stripped of her teacher status and forced to sit near the back of the class wearing a dunce cap.

You'll never guess what she'd been replaced by. An alien! You weren't expecting *that*, were you?

Oh. You were. Fair enough, then.

Arty flapped the neck of his T-shirt back and forth, and squelched as he shifted in his seat. "It's so hot," he panted. "I wish they'd turn those pods down a bit."

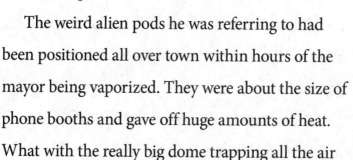

The weird alien pods he was referring to had been positioned all over town within hours of the mayor being vaporized. They were about the size of phone booths and gave off huge amounts of heat. What with the really big dome trapping all the air inside, Sitting Duck had become very warm, very quickly.

"Silence, human," barked one of the aliens who patrolled the class. He wore a brightly colored badge that said "Teaching Assistant," but the children had never seen a teaching assistant with a blaster before.

Arty mimed zipping his mouth closed. The alien nodded its little square head, then continued its patrol around the desks.

At the head of the class, another of the aliens stood on Dribbler's old desk. He clicked the translator button on the side of his helmet and his high-pitched tones squeaked out from behind the dome of glass.

"Today we will continue to fill your minds with all the glory of the Baad-Vaart," he proclaimed in a voice that sounded like he'd been at the Helium. "Witness firsthand the wonder of our home planet, Sulphurius 374."

A hologram beamed from the alien teacher's space suit and suddenly a little alien planet was floating in the middle of the classroom. Gloopy red clouds oozed across its surface, as if its atmosphere was a bit on the jammy side.

The planet became smaller and more worlds came into view, then a sun, then stars, until the image had zoomed out to show off an entire galaxy.

"Sulphurius 374 is located in the Parallax system in the galaxy you know as Andromeda," the alien said. "Using your technology, it would take one-point-seven-million years to reach our world. It took us forty-five minutes to reach yours. This is because we are superior to you in every way."

"Except when it comes to height," Emmie whispered, although she made sure the heavily armed teaching assistant was well out of earshot first.

A Guide to Sulphurius 374

Located in the Parallax Star System (left at the Sun and just keep going), Sulphurius 374 is almost entirely inhospitable to humans, aside from a three-square-mile area near the planet's north pole, which is quite nice this time of year.

Prior to being invaded and colonized by the Baad-Vaart, Sulphurius 374 was known as Lushblue Alpha, and its rolling hills, vast crystal-blue seas, and lovely homemade toffee drew tourists from far and wide across the cosmos.

All that changed when the Baad-Vaart moved in and started mucking the place up, just as they had done with the previous 373 planets they had conquered, after they accidentally left the iron on and burned their original home-world to the ground.

Nowadays it is a forbidding place filled with choking smoke, billowing gas, and not a toffee in sight. Tourism is down by 80 percent, and while this does increase your chances of finding a quiet spot at the beach, stepping onto the sand will incinerate you immediately, which is not what you're after on vacation, really, is it?

"Any questions?" asked the teacher.

"Can we turn the heat down?" asked Arty.

"Negative."

"Is it really hot on your planet, then?" asked Sam. "Is that why all the clouds were red?"

"The temperature on Sulphurius 374 is not hot. It is a perfect five-hundred-and-seventy degrees," said the ET teacher. "It is this planet that is too cold."

Arty gasped. "Five-hundred-and-seventy degrees! That'll cook us alive."

"Affirmative," said the alien. "Your inferior Earth physiology will not permit you to survive in such conditions."

"So why are you keeping us alive, if you're just going to cook us?" Emmie snapped.

"You will serve us until you expire. You will help us make Sitting Duck our main base of operations, from which we shall conquer the entire world," the alien said. Then he shrugged. "Besides, it's how you Earthlings say, a 'laugh'?"

"Oh yeah, hilarious!" Emmie scowled, standing up and slamming her hands down on the desk. Sam grabbed her by the sleeve and tried to pull her back into her seat.

"Calm down," he urged as the pitter-patter of tiny feet told him the teaching assistant was on his way.

"You're going to get into trouble," whimpered Arty.

"Trouble?" Emmie snorted. "We're going to be roasted alive by tiny aliens. How much more trouble can we be in?"

"Silence!" chittered the teaching assistant, skidding around Emmie's desk with his gun

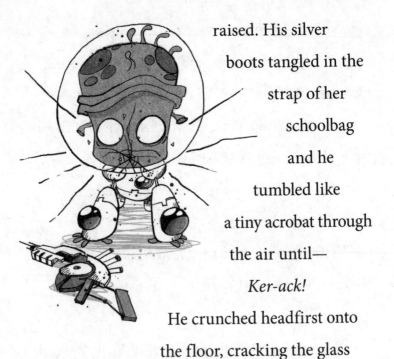

raised. His silver boots tangled in the strap of her schoolbag and he tumbled like a tiny acrobat through the air until—

Ker-ack!

He crunched headfirst onto the floor, cracking the glass of his space helmet. The alien's eyes crossed as they tried to focus on the line running all the way across the fishbowl-like dome. There was silence in the classroom, broken eventually by the sound of the extraterrestrial teaching assistant swallowing nervously.

"Oh," he said, at last. "Not good. I'm, uh . . . just running to the nurse's office."

He ran, screaming his little lungs out, zigzagging through the door and into the corridor. A loud hissing sound followed him from the room, and his silver space suit seemed to swell as he vanished around the doorframe and out of sight.

"Nothing to see," said the teacher, trying to draw the students' attention back to the front of the class. "Everything's normal. Everything's fine."

There was a loud *pop* from the corridor, as if someone had just kissed good-bye to the world's largest balloon. It sounded like something gooey had splattered across the wall; a weird noxious gas drifted into the classroom.

"Nothing to see," the teacher repeated. "Everything's absolutely normal."

"Oh no!" wailed a voice from the corridor. "Klaag's just exploded!"

"Everything's fine," the teacher continued, although even he was starting to sound like he didn't believe it.

As the alien continued its attempt to convince the class that nothing had happened, Sam, Arty, and Emmie leaned closer together.

"Did you see that?" Sam whispered. "One tiny crack and *bang*."

"But why?" Emmie asked. "Why did he explode?"

"I'm not sure," Sam admitted. "But I think it's time we found out."

Backpack Supplies for an Alien Invasion

Good:

- Cloaking technology

- A family-sized pack of tortilla chips

- Anti-ray-gun thermo shielding

- Spaceship security overrides

- Interstellar communication device

- UFO-tracking missile launcher

- Jet-fired rocket boots

Bad:

- A roller skate with one wonky wheel

- Half-set concrete

- Human-tracking missile launcher

- A wind-up monkey

- A pound of colored-pencil shavings

CHAPTER NINE

When the end-of-day bell rang, Sam and the others filed out with the rest of the students, but as soon as the alien teachers weren't looking they ducked behind a stack of chairs and waited for the aliens to leave.

"I think the coast's clear," said Arty as the front door swung closed. He started to stand, but Sam and Emmie dragged him back down just as two more of the little aliens turned the corner.

All three of them held their breath as the ETs trotted by less than a yard from where they were hiding.

"I'm fed up with this helmet," one of them complained. "It looks stupid. One of the Earth children pretended I was a crystal ball earlier and said he could use me to see the future."

"What did you do?"

"Vaporized him. He didn't see that one coming."

"We must be more careful," the second alien said. "After what happened to Klaag today, we cannot afford to take any chances. Not until the atmosphere has been completely converted. Only then will Quarg send the signal from the mother ship to deactivate the helmets."

Behind the stack of chairs, a trickle of sweat tickled down the length of Arty's nose. He twitched. He sniffed. The tickling got worse. There was no way he could stop it. He was going to sneeze!

"Aaah . . ." he began. Sam's and Emmie's eyes widened in horror. The aliens had moved past their hiding place now, but they were still *just*

right there, not yet at the door. One snot explosion
from Arty and the game was up.

"Aaah . . ."

Sam and Emmie frantically shook their heads.

"No!" mouthed Emmie.

"Don't!" mouthed Sam.

"*Aaah . . .*"

There was nothing else for it. Sam clamped
a hand over Arty's nose and mouth just as the
sneeze began to erupt. The effect was like a bomb

going off inside Arty's head. His eyes bulged. His cheeks expanded. And Sam was sure he saw a little bit of snot come flying out of his friend's ear.

Along the corridor, the door clattered closed as the last two aliens headed out of school. Sam and Emmie breathed sighs of relief.

"Wow," said Sam. "That was close."

"*AAATCHOOOO!*"

"Oh, you just had to, didn't you?" Emmie sighed. The door at the end of the corridor was thrown open once again. "You couldn't have waited five more seconds!"

"Run!" yelped Sam as a blast of energy turned the chairs to dust.

Ducking and dodging, the three friends dashed along the corridor away from the aliens. They barreled around a corner, pushed through a fire exit, and ran out into a crowd of students all waiting for the school bus to take them home.

Keeping their heads down, Sam and the others mingled with the line. The two aliens appeared in the doorway behind them, their guns raised. They studied the waiting children for a moment, their fingers hovering over the triggers of their weapons.

Then, with a shrug of their stubby shoulders, they lowered the guns and turned away, pulling the emergency exit closed behind them.

"Well, that was fun," said Sam. "But we should get out of here in case they come looking for us again."

Arty nodded. "Yeah, suppose we should go home."

"We should," agreed Sam. "But we aren't."

☆ ☆ ☆

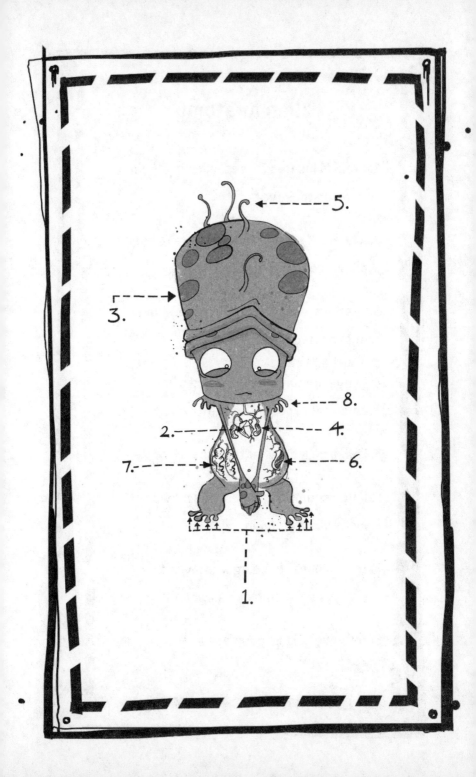

Alien Anatomy

1. Brain is located in toes, allowing them to think on their feet.

2. A heart of stone, so they can take over a planet completely guilt-free.

3. Leathery skin offers protection from unexpected Grazzle-fly bites.

4. Lungs are tiny and shriveled after constant exposure to sulfur gases.

5. I have no idea what that does.

6. If you squint your eyes, this bit sort of looks like a penguin.

7. Two spleens for doing whatever it is spleens do, only twice as well.

8. Your guess is as good as mine.

The wooden floorboards of the tree house creaked nervously as Sam, Emmie, and Arty hunkered down inside. Out through the window, up above the houses, they could see the giant alien spaceship in the center of town. A stem of purple light sprouted from the top, before spreading out to form the dome that kept Sitting Duck trapped.

It was still possible to see through the flickering surface of the dome, and for the first few days the whole thing had been surrounded by the world's media. Over the rest of the week the reporters had started to get a bit fed up, and by the end there was only one journalist left. He wasn't even a proper journalist—he'd just found a notebook in a bin— but he was doing his best and that's what counts.

"Well, that was a good day," said Sam.

Arty stared at him. "Good? We nearly got blasted to bits!"

"And whose fault was that?" Emmie tutted. "But he's right, getting shot at does not make for a particularly good day."

"Ah, but now we know something we didn't know yesterday," Sam said. "We know the aliens have a weakness. We know they don't like our atmosphere. And more important, we know our atmosphere doesn't like them!"

Arty smiled. "And Tribbler the Dribbler said you never paid attention in class!"

"I know! Who knew science lessons might actually be useful?" said Sam. "Now we just have to figure out how to expose them to our atmosphere, and our old friend oxygen should take care of the rest."

"The spaceship," Emmie said. "At the school, those aliens said the ship would send a signal to open the helmets. The ship destroyed the Town Hall."

"It's also creating the force field," Arty added. "It could be the source of all their power."

"You might be right," said Sam, all thoughtful like. "You know what this means, though."

"That we're all going to go home, have a nice cup of tea, and not get into any trouble whatsoever," said Arty hopefully.

"Sort of," said Sam. "Only the exact opposite. No one can get in here to rescue us. The mayor's gone, not that he was much use to begin with. Everyone else is too scared of being blasted to bits to leave their homes."

"Oh, I wonder why," Arty said.

"We're on our own," Sam said. "Help isn't

coming. If we want to stop the aliens before they cook us alive, we're going to have to do it ourselves. Who's with me?"

"I am," said Emmie.

"I'm not," said Arty. He caught the looks from the other two, then gave a sweaty, squelchy sigh. "Fine, I'll come," he said. "But if I get zapped, cooked, or probed *anywhere*, you two are never coming to one of my birthday parties ever again."

Emmie smirked. "Promise?"

☆ ☆ ☆

That night darkness fell across Sitting Duck, just like it did every other night, because that's the whole point of nighttime, isn't it?

As the aliens patrolled the streets, enforcing the evening curfew, three familiar figures crept down the trunk of an old oak tree and tiptoed through the gloom. The purple glow of the dome cast strange scratchy shadows across the ground as Sam, Arty, and Emmie crept like a gang of sneaks through the town.

Making their way through the streets took ages. Aliens marched down every road, pointing their guns at shadows and peering in windows to make sure everyone was tucked up inside where they were supposed to be. Or, at least, they tried to peer in windows, but with them being so small it involved quite a lot of climbing and they only managed about one window in five.

Sam and the others emerged from the alleyway between the pie shop and the hat museum. A blast of heat drove them back. One of the pods lay directly ahead of them, glowing red as it pumped

out choking clouds of crimson smoke, just like the atmosphere on Sulphurius 374.

The sulfurous smog swirled into their lungs, making them hack and splutter and cough. Covering their mouths with their sleeves, they backtracked until the air became cleaner. It wouldn't be long before they couldn't breathe at all.

"Well, the good news is I don't think we're

going to be cooked alive," wheezed Arty. "We'll all be suffocated long before then."

"Oh, well, that is a relief," said Emmie.

Steering clear of any more of the pods, the three friends finally found their way to the back of the building formerly known as the Town Hall and crouched behind the rubble.

They peered across the road to where a long silver ladder led up to a hatch at the base of the giant mother ship.

"It must be using too much energy to maintain the force field," Arty whispered. "So it doesn't have enough left to beam the aliens up and down."

"So their power isn't limitless after all," Sam said, then he let out a sudden gasp of shock as he spotted three aliens standing one on top of the other just a short distance away from the ladder.

It wasn't the sight of the aliens that had shocked Sam, though. It was the sight of whom they were talking to.

"Is that . . . ?"

"Stella," yelped Arty, and Emmie had to clamp a hand over his mouth to stop him from giving them away. "What's she doing here?" he whispered, when Emmie eventually released her grip.

"It looks like she's talking to them," Sam said.

"It all looks very friendly," Emmie said. "What if she's working with them?"

"She wouldn't," said Arty. "Would she?"

A moment later, Stella answered that question herself. With a high-pitched girly giggle, she took hold of the topmost alien's hand and gave it a shake. Then, at a gesture from the ETs, Stella took hold of the bottom rung of the ladder and began to climb.

CHAPTER TEN

Emmie paced back and forth, angrier than a wasp with road rage. "The traitor," she said. "I can't believe she's sold out her own species to a load of alien invaders."

"She always said she'd like to make contact with beings from outer space," said Arty.

"Make contact, yeah, not make best buddies," Emmie said. "Just wait until I get my hands on her. She'll have the biggest black eyes anyone has ever seen!"

"We need to get inside," Sam pointed out. One of the aliens had clambered up the ladder after Stella, but two still hung about like a bad smell, poking anything that moved.

"How do we get past them?" Emmie asked.

Arty pondered. He was good at pondering. If they ever have an Olympics for pondering, Arty will be up there in the medals. "With a neuro-synaptic transmitter I could temporarily disable their visual cortex, allowing us to sneak past."

"Brilliant!" said Sam. "Do it."

"I don't have a neuro-synaptic transmitter."

"Well, can you get one?" asked Emmie.

Arty shook his head. "No."

"Why not?"

"There's no such thing as a neuro-synaptic transmitter," Arty said. "But, you know, if there was it'd be really handy right now."

Emmie stared at him. For a very long time she just stared. "Useless," she said at last. "Absolutely useless."

"I don't see you coming up with any brilliant ideas," Arty sniffed.

Sam looked up at the mother ship, then down at the aliens. Finally, he looked around at the town. *His* town. He loved Sitting Duck. Oh sure, it was full of weirdos, the shops were mostly terrible, and things kept trying to kill him, but he loved it all the same, and there was no way he was letting it fall to an alien invasion. Not today.

"I've got an idea," said Sam. Emmie and Arty turned to look at him.

"Oh yeah? What is it?" asked Emmie.

Sam winked at them. "This," he said, then he turned and ran straight for the aliens. "Coo-ee!" he cried. "Catch me if you can!"

A barrage of blaster fire

erupted around him, and Sam dived out of their path. He was off and running almost at once, zigging and zagging to avoid the laser fire as the aliens gave chase on their stumpy little legs.

"Get back here so we can shoot you!" bellowed one of the aliens.

"Well, that's not going to work now, is it?" scolded the other. "He means come back so we can be *friends*," it called, but Sam was sprinting away and it took all their energy to try to keep up.

"The idiot!" hissed Emmie, when Sam and his pursuers were out of sight. "He's going to get himself killed."

"Maybe," Arty agreed. "But he's not an idiot. He's bought us some time. The ladder's clear. We can go up."

Emmie followed Arty's gaze. The base of the

ladder was completely alien-free. "Hmph," she grunted. "He's still an idiot."

Arty stared up at the massive saucer hanging in the air above them. He swallowed nervously. "So . . . are we going to do this, then?" he asked, but then he realized he was talking to himself. Emmie was already several rungs up the ladder and climbing fast.

"Well, come on then," she hissed. "We haven't got all night!"

The inside of the spaceship looked exactly like the inside

of a spaceship. Lights blinked on and off along the chrome-colored walls. Doors went *sssht* and opened at their approach. Strange alien symbols hung down from the ceiling, including one that Emmie couldn't help but think looked like a tiny cowboy riding a cat.

The farther they went into the ship, the darker and less polished it became. The shiny walls turned to dull black metal. Brass pipes snaked along the ceiling, with something wet and gloopy-sounding bubbling along inside.

Steam rose through vents in the floor, and every surface seemed to shiver and vibrate as Arty and Emmie crept stealthily by.

"Do you have any idea where we're going?" Emmie whispered as they rounded another bend and waited for a door to hurl itself open.

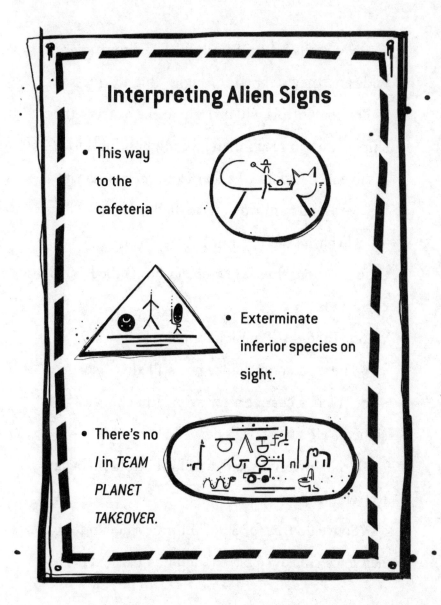

Interpreting Alien Signs

- This way to the cafeteria

- Exterminate inferior species on sight.

- There's no *I* in *TEAM PLANET TAKEOVER.*

"Not really," Arty admitted. The door *clanged* wide and they stepped through. "But my guess is the main controls will be right at the heart of the ship. If we can reach there, we might be able to disable it." He dabbed a tear from the corner of his eye. "And Sam won't have died in vain."

"He hasn't died!" Emmie barked. She thought about this. "He *probably* hasn't died," she corrected.

She thought about it a moment longer.

"There's a good chance he's still alive," she said. "Well, a chance anyway. A slim chance." She sighed. "He's toast, isn't he?"

"Probably," Arty said, and his bottom lip began to tremble.

"So we do this for Sam," Emmie said, and even her voice cracked a bit, though if you asked her she'd say it was from the heat and the steam and all that stuff. "Okay?"

Arty nodded. "For Sam," he said, then another door *slammed* open and there, before them, was Stella Gazey.

She stood at a control terminal in the center of a large round room, tapping keys like they were going out of fashion. Stella looked up as Arty and Emmie entered, and her eyes reached dizzying new widths of wideness.

"What on Earth are you two doing here?" she gasped.

"I don't even know how you can bring yourself to say that word," said Emmie, cracking her knuckles menacingly.

Stella frowned. "What, 'here'?"

"No, of course not 'here'," Emmie snapped. "You

wouldn't get very far not being able to say 'here,' would you? I meant '*Earth.*' I don't know how you can say it after you betrayed it the way you have."

"No I haven't," said Stella.

"Yes you have—look." Emmie pointed to Stella's fingers, which were still dancing across the keys.

"Oh, *that!*" said Stella. "I can see why you might be confused."

"I'm not confused," Emmie said. "*You're* confused."

"You're confused about being confused," insisted Stella.

"The only confusing thing around here is how confused you are about me being confused about being confused," Emmie said.

Arty tried to make sense of that last sentence,

but only succeeded in giving himself a nosebleed.
He butted in before the other two could carry on.

"So . . . if you haven't betrayed the Earth, what
are you doing here?" he asked.

Stella smiled nervously. "Sabotage!" she said.
"I've tricked the little blighters, y'see? I told them
I was offering myself up for experimentation.
Aliens love a bit of that. They think they can just
come down here and shoot our mayor and steal
our planet. It's not cool!"

Her fingers clacked across the keyboard.
"Almost done," she said. "Any moment and I'll
have complete command of this ship. All I have to
do is . . . Oh dear."

"Oh dear?" Emmie said. "What do you mean
'oh dear'?"

Stella hit a key and a holographic display

blinked into life between them. It looked like a
computer screen just hanging around in the air
paying gravity no heed whatsoever. A number of
cryptic alien symbols flashed up on the display.

"What does it say?" Arty asked.

"Hang on, I think I can get it to translate,"
Stella said. She began tapping buttons that
floated in the air beside the symbols. As Emmie
and Arty watched, the shapes began to shift and
change until they formed a word.

"Drowssap?" said Emmie. "What's that
supposed to mean?"

"We're on the wrong side of the hologram,"
Arty pointed out. "We're seeing it backward."

"It says *password*," Stella said, and a flicker
of worry darted across her face. She looked
through the screen and met Arty's gaze. "Don't

suppose you have any experience in cracking codes, do you?"

Arty flexed his fingers and shot Emmie a *told-you-so* sort of look. "You know," he said, "it's funny you should ask."

CHAPTER ELEVEN

Arty was quickly coming to realize that it was much easier to crack a code when you actually had a code to crack. Inside the password box were three shapes: a triangle, a heptagon, and a square—that was it.

"Try *password*," Emmie suggested. "It's always that."

Stella typed the word *password*. The screen flickered red and made a sound like a buzzer from a TV talent show.

"It won't be that obvious," Arty said. "Try *aliens*."

Stella typed. The screen went red. The buzzer buzzed.

"*Baad-Vaart*," said Emmie.

"*Andromeda*," said Arty.

"*Quarg*," they said together.

Stella typed all three, but all three were wrong.

"What about . . . I don't know . . . *one-two-three-four*?" Emmie said.

Stella typed. The screen went red and on came that buzzer again.

"Not it," she said.

"Still," said Arty, "at least all these failed attempts haven't triggered some sort of alarm."

Some sort of alarm suddenly triggered. The lights in the room dipped to an ominous shade of red as sirens wailed throughout the ship.

"One day you'll learn to keep your mouth shut," said Emmie, shaking her head in disgust.

"They'll be here any minute," Stella fretted. "We should run, get out, get away!"

"No way," growled Emmie. "We need to crack this and we're not leaving here until we do."

"Maybe you were onto something," said Arty. "With the numbers, I mean. Their initial message to us, it was all numbers, wasn't it? Maybe the password is, too."

"What's the name of their planet again?" Emmie asked. "Sulphurius . . . something. What was the number?"

"Three-seven-four, of course!" Arty cried. "That's

what the shapes are all about. It's the number of sides on a triangle, a heptagon, and a square."

He elbowed Stella away from the keyboard and hammered in the digits one after the other. The screen flashed red, but they couldn't hear the buzzing over the scream of the alarms.

He punched the keys again.

3

7

4

He stopped.

He stared.

He sweated.

For a moment, nothing seemed to happen, but then the screen flickered green and the room was filled by a circle of holographic screens. The displays encircled them like a record-breaking doughnut, displaying digits and symbols and maps and other fancy stuff like that.

"We did it!" Arty shouted.

"I can't believe your dorky treasure hunt and code breaking paid off!" Emmie said.

"I told you it was a good birthday present! Look, are those the gas pods?" asked Arty, pointing to a display that showed one of the devices in action.

"And this looks like the force field on this one," added Emmie.

"We did it," breathed Stella. "From here we can undo the damage. We can fix this!"

Her fingers were back on the keys, tapping and clicking and clacking in a blinding blur of keyboard skills. As Arty watched, the on-screen pod stopped glowing and became dark. The smoke, which had been hissing from it, curled lazily off on the breeze.

"Pods deactivated!" he yelped.

"Get the shield down!" Emmie cried. "Quick, before the Baad-Vaarts get here!"

"I'm working on it," Stella replied. She tippity-tapped like a madwoman, until smoke poured from between the keys. "Almost . . . done." She jabbed a finger against a final key and Emmie watched the force field fizzle out of existence.

Arty and Emmie whooped with delight. "You did it!" Arty cried.

"*We* did it," Stella corrected. "I couldn't have done it without you two."

Emmie shuffled uncomfortably. "I'm . . . I'm sorry I doubted you," she said. "I'm sorry I thought you'd betrayed us."

Stella winked one massively magnified eye.

"Think nothing of it. I just hope now that we can be friends."

"Yeah, of course," smiled Emmie.

"Excellent!" laughed Stella.

And then she exploded.

How to Be an Alien Resistance Fighter

Want to join the resistance against the Baad-Vaart? Check out our strict requirements below to see if you've got what it takes.

1. **Must Resist Aliens.** This is a key requirement. We do not have time to waste on Alien Resistance Fighters who are unwilling or unable to resist aliens.

2. **Must Fight Aliens.** Again, very important. Resisting aliens is all well and good, but to be a true Alien Resistance *Fighter* the fighting bit is pretty vital, too. That's why we put it in the name.

3. **Aliens Are NOT Allowed.** Only members of the human race are eligible to become

Alien Resistance Fighters. Or animals, I suppose. Yeah, only human beings or animals. If you're an alien then I'm sorry, you cannot become a member.

4. **Must Be Brave and/or Stupid.** From sneaking on board alien spaceships to climbing down the gullet of a Flarglewhapian Slime Beast, the life of an Alien Resistance Fighter is often dangerous and usually short. Only the bravest or most dim-witted should apply.

5. **Must Have Own Uniform.** Sorry, we are unable to supply uniforms at this time. However, badges may be purchased from your direct superior for a nominal fee. Terms and conditions apply.

CHAPTER TWELVE

One moment Stella was there; the next she was a small pile of colorful dust on the floor. Her glasses landed in the dust pile with a soft *plop*, their massive lenses melted and warped.

"S-Stella?" Arty whimpered, although what he was hoping for was anyone's guess. Stella was in no condition to reply. Or to do much else, for that matter, except maybe act as cat litter.

"Oh dear, and you came so close," squeaked Quarg, toddling into the room on his teeny-tiny legs, a small band of aliens in his wake. Smoke curled from the barrel of his ray gun. He tried blowing it away, but as he was still wearing his space helmet, he just looked a bit stupid.

"You shot her," growled Emmie.

"She tricked her way on board, broke my pods, and lowered my shield," replied Quarg. "So I'd say that makes us even."

The alien commander gestured toward the center of the room with the gun. "Away from the controls, please," he urged. "I don't want any more funny business."

Emmie and Arty shuffled away from the screens, their arms raised, their hands in full view. "You won't get away with this," Emmie warned.

"Oh, but I will. And I am," laughed Quarg.

"The Earth will be terraformed. Your atmosphere shall be replaced. Every living Earth creature will die most agonizing deaths, and there is nothing—let me say that again so I make myself quite clear—*nothing* that you can do about it."

Quarg stepped closer to them, but not close enough for Emmie to make a grab for him. She kept her hands raised, waiting for her chance to strike.

"I am not an unkind evil alien warlord," Quarg said. "So I'm going to be generous."

"You're going to let us go?" asked Arty.

"No. I'm going to kill you both right here and now." He raised the gun and aimed it right between Arty's eyes. "Don't say I'm not good to you. Any last grauak?"

Arty blinked in surprise. "Any last what?"

"Gerumk," coughed Quarg. He dropped his gun and pressed his hands against the side of his helmet. "Umffark! Nooooooo!"

With a hiss and a click, Quarg's helmet snapped back into his suit. The alien's stubby fingers clutched at his throat as his head began to swell like a rapidly inflating balloon. His fellow aliens looked equally uncomfortable.

Arty and Emmie both stepped back. "This is going to get messy," Emmie warned.

"You can say that again," said a voice from behind them. They turned to see Sam standing by the control panel. On-screen, a diagram of a Baad-Vaart space helmet flashed on and off.

"You're alive!" cheered Emmie.

"Of course I'm alive. All I had to do was outrun some pesky tiny aliens. And once they

heard the alarm, I slipped onto the UFO right
behind them."

"Told you he'd be fine," grinned Arty. He turned
back to Quarg and the others, who were now roughly
the shape of beach balls, and getting rounder all
the time. "Now what do we do about . . . ?"

Bang!

Soggy chunks of exploded alien splattered
across the room, caking the friends from head to

toe. Silently, they wiped the oozy blue goo from their eyes, and then staggered as the ship was rocked by a series of gloopy *pops.*

"I think we should probably run," Sam suggested.

"Yeah, I think you're probably right," Emmie agreed. "What do you think, Arty?"

But this time it was Arty who was already on the move. He hurled himself through the door and they heard his voice echo back at them along the corridor.

"Well what are you waiting for? *Run!*"

They slid down the ladder into a scene of absolute chaos. Humans and aliens alike were running around screaming and waving their arms like teenage girls at a concert by some terrible boy band or other.

The streets were awash with blue sludge. From all directions came the *pop, pop, pop* of exploding

Baad-Vaartians as their protective helmets opened and the Earth's atmosphere took a very firm stance on marauding aliens. Some of the aliens desperately tried to keep their helmets pulled forward as they attempted to get back to the spaceship.

Just as Sam and the others reached the ground, the ladder began to retract back up into the ship. A few alien stragglers hung on for dear life as their fellow extraterrestrials exploded in a blue goop. The whole spacecraft shuddered violently to one side, and for one terrible moment the trio thought it was going to drop right on their heads, which would have been a really depressing end to the story.

But probably quite a funny ending, too, now that I think about it. Anyway, it didn't do that. It just lurched about for a bit, then with a final Earth-evacuating launch-spin it rocketed upward toward the vast abyss of space. The leaderless alien survivors made an embarrassed exit out of Earth's atmosphere.

Sam, Emmie, and Arty watched the spaceship get smaller and smaller. Soon it looked smaller than the Moon. Then it looked smaller than a much smaller Moon. Finally, it looked smaller than them both.

And then, it was gone.

Emmie shook her fist in the direction of the fleeing ship. "And don't come back!"

"I reckon this is one planet they won't be trying to conquer again in a hurry," Sam said.

Arty looked worried. "But what if they do? What if they come back?"

Sam put his arm around his friend's shoulder. "Then we'll be waiting for them, won't we?" he said. "Now come on. Let's go home."

World Conquering: A Guide for Would-Be Alien Warlords

So you've found a planet you'd like to conquer. Congratulations! But what's next? Cut out our pocket-size guide and bring it with you on your next invasion. You'll be crushing those civilizations like the pathetic bugs they are in no time!

1. **Make an Entrance.** Good ways to make an entrance include swooping over the treetops in your flying saucer or beaming down as if from nowhere. Bad ways include falling from your ship's ramp and crash-landing your jet pack into a tree.

2. **Establish a Base of Operations.** Of course you could take over a palace, political

building, or fancy restaurant and use that as your base of operations, but you've already got a much more suitable space available, if you think about it. (Hint: You flew there in it.)

3. **Kill and/or Dominate Native Life-Forms.** It's best to pick and choose which life-forms you elect to kill and/or dominate carefully. On the planet Earth, for example, you'll probably want to focus your attention on the human race as opposed to, say, ducks. Having total control over the planet's duck population is unlikely to be of any lasting benefit.

4. **Adapt the Atmosphere.** The atmospheres of alien worlds may be made up of any number of elements, including argon, helium, jam—and even oxygen.

Temperatures on many worlds are also far below what may be comfortable for us. The careful deployment of terraforming pods will soon have the place warmed up and pumped full of noxious gas, though.

5. **Relax.** You've done all the hard work, now sit back and enjoy the fruits of your labor. Another world is just around the corner waiting to be crushed beneath your fearsome boot, but for now take a minute to savor the screams of the dying native population and congratulate yourself on a job well done.

CHAPTER THIRTEEN

So here we are at the final chapter. All the aliens have either cleared off or exploded into a sticky paste, and everything is right with the world.

Well, mostly everything. There's a bit of an eggy smell hanging about the place, like a fart trapped under a duvet. It'll fade soon enough, though. The Earth's atmosphere is a truly wonderful thing, even if it doesn't have enough jam in it for my liking.

The mayor has still been vaporized, of course, but no one's all that bothered. Half of them have forgotten they ever even had a mayor, and those who do remember him dearly wish that they didn't.

Lots of other people were blasted to bits, too, but let's not dwell too much on them. Let's turn our attention instead to what was until just yesterday the Sitting Duck Observatory, but which is now called . . .

Tell you what, why don't I let Arty tell you? Here he is now with a big pair of scissors, getting ready to cut the ribbon. He's looking all nervous, what with everyone in town (who wasn't horribly killed by aliens) having gathered to watch him.

"For her heroism in the face of danger," Arty said. "For her willingness to risk her own life to save us all. And for her really massive glasses . . ."

A mumble of agreement rippled around the crowd.

"I now name this the Stella Gazey Observatory."

He cut the ribbon. The audience clapped. Arty's mom made him pose for a picture with Sam and Emmie, because she was so proud of them. Then everyone else cleared off back down the hill, leaving Arty alone with Emmie and Sam. Well,

come on, there's loads of cleaning up to do and it's hardly going to do itself, is it?

"Did I do okay?" Arty asked. Sam clapped him on the shoulder.

"You did great."

"Your mom and dad didn't come," Arty said.

"Nah, they still think it was all just a film," said Sam with a shrug. "They think it deserves to win an Oscar."

They all laughed. Parents can be so dim sometimes.

"You were right, you know?" said Emmie. "Stella was pretty cool."

Arty looked up at the telescope towering above them. "Yeah," he smiled. "She really was."

"Except her glasses," Emmie added. "They were weird."

The three walked side by side down the hill.

"We couldn't have done it without her, though," said Arty, and they all nodded at that.

"We couldn't have done it without any of us," Sam said. "Your brains, Emmie's ingenuity . . ."

"And her ability to kick things really hard," Arty added.

"Yeah, and that," grinned Sam.

"What about you? Drawing those aliens away, coming back and turning off their helmets," Emmie said. "You're the real hero here."

"Nah, it took all of us," Sam insisted. "The Three Muskadweebs."

Good grief, this is touching stuff, right? I'm tearing up here. Someone pass me a tissue before I cry all over the page.

"Anyway, I should probably be thanking the aliens," Sam said.

"*Thanking them?*"

"Why?"

"Well thanks to them I'm probably going to pass the next science test. I've got a pretty good idea what it takes to survive in Earth's atmosphere now," he said. "At least, I've got a better idea than they do!"

And with that, Sam, Arty, and Emmie strolled down the hill to Sitting Duck, and they all lived happily ever after.

Actually, now that I come to think about it, they didn't. If anything, things went from bad to worse.

But that, as they say, is another story. . . .

Code Breaking
with Friends

Want to devise foolproof codes that allow you and your friends to communicate without anyone else being able to listen in? Why not try some of the techniques below?

The Movie Name Code: Think of your twenty-six favorite movies, then rank them in order from best to worst. Each movie then represents a letter of the alphabet, allowing you to quickly pass messages unnoticed. For example, the word *Moon* might translate as:

Die Hard—Ghostbusters—
Ghostbusters—Bambi

Quick, easy-to-remember, and utterly foolproof—this method is none of these things, so give it a try today!

The Noises a Bee Might Make Code: This code is simplicity itself to learn, but very difficult to crack. Every word in the dictionary is assigned a noise that a bee might make (e.g. *buzz, bzzz, buuuuzzzz,* etc.) and each sound is memorized by all those who wish to communicate with each other using the code. To untrained ears the code will simply sound like two people making bee noises—but those in the know will be receiving your message loud and clear! Warning: Learning this code will not allow you to talk to bees. That would be stupid.

The Fish Picture Code: Swap every letter in the alphabet with a hand-drawn picture of a fish, each one only slightly different from the others. After that you can't go wrong, really.

**Practice writing codes.
Then practice breaking them!**

Read them all!

Disaster strikes the town of Sitting Duck again . . . and again . . . and again . . .

Available now!

Coming soon!

Read on for a sneaky look at the disaster-defeating wisdom we have coming up for you in the next book . . .

Disaster Diaries: Brainwashed!

Ravenous zombie hordes and swarms of power-hungry tiny aliens are just some of the disasters the town of Sitting Duck has faced.

But danger never sleeps and a new evil genius has arisen, and he's planning world domination with the aid of his homemade brainwashing device! Are Sam, Arty, and Emmie brave enough to save the day for the third time in a row?

If they aren't, everyone—including you, dear reader—will totally lose their minds!

CHAPTER ONE

KABOOM!

No, that wasn't an explosion. Sorry to get your hopes up. An explosion would have been a smashing way to open the book, but that's not what's happening. It was the sound of a thought arriving in the brain of Sam Saunders with such force it was almost loud enough for the people around him to hear it, too.

The thought that *KABOOMED* into his head as he darted across the school playing field was this:

Exercise is excellent.

Now don't get me wrong—Sam isn't one of those weirdos who loves going to the gym and running on treadmills until they throw up all down themselves. The sort of exercise Sam loves is the running-around-with-friends sort. The wind-in-your-face, isn't-it-great-to-be-alive type of activity.

And it's not like he's forcing exercise down anyone's throat. He isn't wearing a T-shirt that says how excellent exercise is or anything. He's just thinking it inside his own head, and there's nothing wrong with that, even if he is thinking it really quite loudly indeed.

Behind him, one of his best friends, Emmie, hurried to keep up. She also enjoyed running around, but not enough to make a *KABOOMED!* noise inside her mind.

Much farther behind Emmie was Sam's other best friend, Arty. From the way he was sweating and panting and dragging his clumping great feet across the grass, it was plain for all to see that physical effort was not really Arty's cup of tea. He did not think exercise was excellent. He thought it was a load of rubbish, make no mistake.

"I'm . . . going . . . to die." Arty wheezed.

Emmie glanced over her shoulder. Arty's face was

red and puffed up, like the wrong end of a baboon, so Emmie offered him some words of encouragement.

"Oh shut up, you're not going to die."

"Almost there, Arty," called Sam. "You can do it!"

Up ahead, across the playing field, he could see a group of kids gathering beside . . . someone else. The sun in his eyes made it impossible to figure out who it was.

Sam and Emmie slowed to a jog so as not to leave Arty trailing too far behind. They're nice like that. And people say youngsters have no consideration these days.

"It's not fair," Arty gasped. "It's bad enough we have to do PE in school, now I'm d-doing sports club during the holidays."

Sports club was Arty's idea of a living nightmare. It was supposedly started to give the young people of

Sitting Duck a fun place to go during the holidays, but Arty reckoned the real reason it was started was to keep them out of trouble. Either that, or the whole thing had been devised as a very elaborate form of torture just for him.

"You'll have a great time!" said Sam.

"I'll have a heart attack," Arty grumbled.

Emmie squinted into the sun as she ran. "Is that Coach Mackenzie?"

"Oh no," Arty groaned. "He made me run until I was sick!"

"How long did that take?" Emmie asked.

"About a minute and a half," Arty wheezed.

Sam shrugged. "He was okay. All those laps he made us do came in handy when we had to run away from the undead. If it wasn't for him, we might have been zombie chow."

"I'd rather be zombie chow than be running laps," Arty said. "Please don't let it be him."

"I don't think it is," said Sam. They were getting closer now and the sun was dipping behind a cloud. "Not unless he's got a lot thinner."

"And become a woman," added Emmie.

"I wouldn't put anything past that guy," Arty muttered.

He stopped running. His body gave him no choice. He hobbled onward, Sam and Emmie slowing down to walk beside him.

"We still going to the Town Hall after this?" Arty asked.

"The Town Hall was blown to smithereens by an alien death ray," Emmie pointed out. "Or did you forget?"

Arty sighed. It was tremendously painful and

he made a mental note not to do it again. "They're rebuilding," he said. "And they're announcing the candidates running for mayor today."

"Why would anyone want to be mayor after what happened to the last one?" Emmie wondered. "Mayor Sozzle was zapped into millions of atoms."

Arty cleared his throat and nodded in Sam's direction. Emmie quickly realized what he was getting at.

"But I . . . erm . . . I'm sure if your dad wins then *he* won't be zapped to atoms," she said to Sam. "I meant the other candidates."

Sam shrugged. "I wouldn't worry about it. The aliens aren't coming back here in a hurry."

"Exactly! Anyway, it's going to be sooooo boring," Emmie complained. "A load of people just standing around talking rubbish about how much better they'll be for Sitting Duck than the rest. How dull can you get?"

"You don't have to come," Sam told her.

"Are you kidding?" cried Emmie. "It's that or I have to go back home and watch Great Aunt Doris chew off her toenails. I wouldn't miss this Town Hall thing for the world."

"Ooh, hello! New people!" beamed the definitely-not-Coach-Mackenzie person. She was a young woman with short blond hair and a smile that could crack walnuts across a crowded room.

Actually, I've got no idea what I mean by that. I was trying to say her smile was very nice. I've got no clue how walnuts got involved.

Her eyes sparkled like lemonade, only blue and round and less runny. She wore gray shorts that showed off her legs, like shorts tend to do, and a white T-shirt with the word *COACH* written across the front.

"You're the most beautiful creature I've ever seen," blurted Arty. Around him, the dozen or so other kids snickered behind their hands. Arty felt his face turn a worrying shade of red. "Er . . . by which I mean 'hello,'" he said.

He held out a shaking hand. The coach flashed him a walnut-cracker and shook it. "Pleased to meet you," she said, and Arty knew in that moment he'd never wash that hand again.

Emmie sneered and turned to Sam. "Can you believe the way he's drooling over her?" she asked, but Sam was staring past her, his head cocked to one side, a smile tugging at the corners of his mouth.

Were he a cartoon, Sam's eyes would have

been the shape of love-hearts, and he'd almost certainly have been floating several inches above the ground. Not being a cartoon, though, he merely stood there with a soppy expression on his face and dribbled very slightly down his chin.

Create a Disaster
Survival Kit

What would you put in
your own Disaster Survival Kit?

Maybe, like Arty, a Bristly-Brain-Basher
(aka toilet brush) is all you need to keep
enemies at bay?

Can you invent a more sophisticated
form of weaponry using a toilet roll or
an empty cookie tin?

Or do you really just want some sweets
and a clean T-shirt?

Pack your bag for the apocalypse and
keep it by the door in case of disaster!

About the Author and Illustrator

R. McGeddon is absolutely sure the world is almost certainly going to probably end very soon. A strange, reclusive fellow—so reclusive, in fact, that no one has ever seen him, not even his mom—he plots his stories using letters cut from old newspapers and types them up on an encrypted typewriter. It's also believed that he goes by other names, including A. Pocalypse and N. Dov Days, but since no one's ever met him in real life, it's hard to say for sure. One thing we know is that when the aliens invade, he'll be ready!

The suspiciously happy, award-winning illustrator **Jamie Littler** hails from the mysterious, mystical southern lands of England. It is said that the only form of nourishment he needs is to draw, which he does on a constant basis. This could explain why his hair grows so fast. When he is not drawing, which is a rare thing indeed, he spends his time trying to find the drawing pen he has just lost. He is down to his last one.